RICK FERTIG

Something wrong . . .

I considered the possibilities. It was all right
to have any of those ordinary ailments that
struck you down for a little while and let you
bounce back up again. But I was certain now
that I had something that didn't just go away.
There was something wrong with me that set
me apart from everyone at the party, from all
the people I had ever known.

Other Apple Paperbacks you will want to read:

No Place for Me
by Barthe DeClements

With You and Without You
by Ann M. Martin

You, Me, and Gracie Makes Three
by Dean Marney

The Secret Diary of Katie Dinkerhoff
by Lila Perl

I Thought You Were My Best Friend
by Ann Reit

ONE STEP AT A TIME

Deborah Kent

AN
APPLE
PAPERBACK

SCHOLASTIC INC.
New York Toronto London Auckland Sydney

ISBN 0-590-41580-8

12 11 10 9 8 7 6 5 4 3 2 1   9/8 0 1 2 3 4/9

Printed in the U.S.A.   01

First Scholastic printing, September 1989

ONE STEP AT A TIME

Chapter 1

"For tomorrow, I'd like you to do the exercises on page 14 of your English grammar book," Mrs. Blanchard explained. "And I'll look forward to reading your compositions on Monday. Three hundred words on your favorite movie."

I'd never heard a teacher pile on the homework so politely. It didn't help. Already I felt as though I were being buried under a landslide of assignments. You might think they'd have a little mercy on our very first day of high school.

The bell rang, and the long day was finally over. I gathered up my books and joined the stampede for the door. Somebody loomed up suddenly in front of me, and I barely missed a collision. It seemed like that's what high school was all about — work and more work, people and more people, crushing in on me from every side.

"Tracy Newbury?"

The sound of my name jolted me to a stop. I spun around to find Mrs. Blanchard studying me, her lips curved in a faint, sweet smile. Somehow whenever a teacher called me back unexpectedly like that, smile or no smile, my heart started thumping as if I were in trouble.

"Are you by any chance related to Melissa Newbury?" Mrs. Blanchard asked, and I knew my instincts had been correct. Trouble was coming all right, and it was of the first magnitude.

"Yeah," I admitted. "She's my sister."

Mrs. Blanchard's smile blossomed across her whole face. "Your sister! You must be so proud of her! She's the most brilliant student I ever taught. How does she manage all her subjects, plus her practicing?"

"I don't know," I said. The room was nearly empty by now, and I gazed longingly at the door.

But Mrs. Blanchard wasn't through yet. "When she played at the spring concert last year, she brought tears to my eyes. The violin is such a beautiful instrument, and she plays it like an angel! How much time does she spend practicing?"

2

That was one of the questions people always asked about Melissa. I pulled out the standard answer. "About four hours a day. Sundays she takes a vacation and only works for two hours."

"It's just marvelous, that kind of dedication," Mrs. Blanchard said. "I'm delighted to have another Newbury girl in my class this year. Are you musical, too?"

I shook my head. "I can't carry a tune in a bucket," I said, summoning a laugh, as though it didn't really matter.

"Well, I bet you have other talents. I can't wait to read your composition. Melissa used to write the most wonderful essays."

It was time for Standard Comment Number Two. "She's good at just about anything she tries."

"And I'm sure you are, too," Mrs. Blanchard exclaimed. She looked old, maybe ten years older than my mother, with fuzzy gray hair and a baggy blue dress and really clunky black shoes. She had the kind of voice that cracked when she got excited. Talking about Melissa made it crack a lot.

She picked up an eraser and began to wipe the front blackboard. "I better get going," I said. "Bye."

"Say hello to Melissa for me," Mrs. Blanchard said. "Tell her to drop by and see me one of these days, if she has the time."

"Okay," I said, and made my escape.

I wondered how long it would take for Mrs. Blanchard to realize that the only thing Melissa and I had in common was our last name. I had no dazzling talent in music, or in anything else. At school my very best work was just average compared to my sister's. I even *looked* unremarkable. People passed me on the street without a second glance at my ordinary face and my straight brown hair, but one glimpse of Melissa — blonde and elegantly slender — stopped them short.

I'd promised to meet Brenda by my locker right after school — if I could *find* my locker. The two of us had been inseparable since sixth grade. We always shared everything, from our desserts to our deepest secrets. It was hard to fathom how we would survive high school, now that phys ed was our only class together.

My locker was in the basement — at least I remembered that much. But once I emerged from the stairwell, I had no idea which way to go. I started off to the right, down a long hall where locker doors clanged and little clusters of kids talked and laughed. I knew that my locker was near Room 28, but the numbers on the doors were hard to read in the dim light. I made out 11 and 13, and finally passed a woodworking shop, which was definitely unfamiliar. Disgusted, I turned around and headed back the way I had come.

The corridor branched just beyond the stairway. A couple of the overhead lights must have been burned out, because the hall around the corner wasn't just dim, it was almost pitch dark. My locker had to be down there somewhere, but I'd never be able to recognize it. Nobody could see anything in a place like that. Maybe Brenda and I could meet right out here, where there was enough light for us to see each other.

"Brenda?" I called, but there was no answer.

Cautiously I stepped forward, waiting for my eyes to grow accustomed to the gloom. But the darkness was thicker the farther I went. I inched along through a dense fog without a clue where I was going.

From somewhere up ahead came an eerie, hollow slam, and the heavy jangle of keys. The skin prickled on the back of my neck. Into my mind sprang an image from a horror film I'd watched on HBO the night before — a bloody hand slowly reaching out through the doorway.

I wanted to whirl and run, and in an instant of pure panic I knew that in this darkness I could only stumble and fall in a helpless heap. I pressed against the wall as slow, ominous footsteps drew closer. At any moment a cold hand would clutch my throat, choking off my rising scream. . . .

"Good night," said a man's tired voice. A vague figure rose beside me, swinging something large and square that had to be a briefcase. Then it was gone, the footsteps receding into the distance. It was no phantom of the underworld, only one of the teachers, closing up for the day. I leaned against the wall, my heart racing, swept by a tide of crazy relief.

"Tracy! There you are! What took you so long?"

"Brenda! You're here!" I couldn't see the human behind the voice, but I rushed toward the wonderful sound of her. In a moment I made out her small, slender form as she hurried to meet me.

"What happened?" Brenda asked. "I've been waiting fifteen minutes."

She sounded so unruffled, as though the dark corridor didn't even faze her. "I got hung up with my English teacher," I said lightly. "She had Melissa a couple of years ago."

Brenda knew exactly what I meant. "Oh, yuck!" she groaned. "She kept you all that time? I thought maybe you got lost or something."

"Well, who wouldn't, in a place like this?" I

said. "It sure is creepy down here! Someone came walking toward me a minute ago and I almost screamed bloody murder!"

"It is a little spooky," Brenda agreed. "Get your stuff and let's go."

"Yeah, sure," I said. "Even if I can find my locker, how am I supposed to do the stupid combination in the dark?"

Brenda giggled, as if she thought I were only kidding. But I just stood there, not making a move. "Come on," she urged. "Where's that slip they handed out, with your combination on it?"

I rummaged in my purse, but I wouldn't be able to read the slip even if I found it. "Forget it," I said. "I don't need anything anyway. I've already got my books for tonight."

"What about your jacket?" Brenda insisted.

"It'll be warm out."

"Yeah, but it might be cold tomorrow morning," she reminded me.

Sometimes Brenda was so practical I couldn't stand it. "It's today," I said impatiently. "I'll worry about tomorrow tomorrow. Let's get out of here."

"The stairway over there leads to the outside," Brenda said. I saw the gesture of her pointing hand, but the stairway was hidden in the shadows.

"How do you know?" I asked, setting out after her. "How come you know where you're going down here?"

It was Brenda's turn to sound impatient. "It's not *that* dark. I mean, you don't have to make such a big deal out of it!"

"Well — " I began, but something warned me to let the topic drop. I followed her up an echoing flight of stairs, running my hand along the banister as we went. At the top Brenda pushed open a door, and a great blaze of light burst in upon us. The brightness was so sudden and intense that I reeled back, clutching the railing to keep my balance.

Holding the door wide, Brenda glanced at me in surprise. "Coming?" she inquired.

"Sure," I said. But I waited another second or two while my eyes adjusted to the novelty of sunshine. At last, when the ground lay clearly before my feet, I stepped out onto the sidewalk.

I knew precisely where I was now. Off to the right lay the football field, and to the left stretched a sea of parking lots. Pretty soon the maze of school corridors would feel as predictable as the warm, sunny world outside.

"There's the cutest boy in my algebra class," Brenda was saying. "He sits right across from me. He was helping the teacher pass out books, and when he walked by my desk he looked over at me and he kind of winked. He's got these big blue eyes, and real blond hair, kind of curly — I don't know how I'll ever hear a word about math in there!"

"The most exciting thing that happened in my algebra class was the teacher dropped this whole big stack of xeroxed sheets, and they went all over the floor," I said. "We'd been sitting there through half an hour of all this boring junk about number sets or something, and then *kaboom!* Everybody cracked up!"

Each story led to another as we crossed the parking lot and started along Hancock Avenue. Brenda swore that her English teacher had orange hair and wore eye shadow an inch thick. I described my social studies teacher, who gave us a drill sergeant's speech about how the namby-pamby days of grammar school were over. Brenda said he was the one in charge of her study hall, where he patrolled the aisles muttering, "No gum-chewing! . . . Absolutely no talking! . . . Did I hear a radio?"

But all the time we talked, I couldn't shake the feeling of terror that had gripped me in the dark basement hallway. That teacher with the briefcase hadn't had any trouble finding his way out. He and Brenda had each spotted me long before I saw them. Did they have eyes like cats, that worked in pitch blackness? Why had I alone been so utterly lost?

At the end of Hancock we reached the patch of woods behind Brenda's house. We called our good-byes, and she disappeared among the trees on the shortcut path up to her backyard. Slowly I turned away and headed down Hickory Road to our house.

I could have found our driveway even in the dead of night, by the barking of the dogs. Dad had designed the kennel so the runs all looked out over the woods, hoping the dogs wouldn't spend all their time watching for cars on the road. Mom always said his kennel was absolutely perfect in design, but the dogs still exploded into a frenzy of barking whenever anyone came up to the house.

My mother raises purebred German shepherds. She started out with just two dogs, Gretchen and Algonquin, and when they had pups she entered one of them in a dog show. After two years the project had expanded so much she and Dad decided we should move out to the country, even though it meant they had to drive Melissa an extra forty-five minutes each way to her violin lessons. When I was in sixth grade we moved out here to Millbrook in the hills of Sussex County, New Jersey.

Now my steps quickened as I heard Algonquin's deep rumble, the joyful greetings of Gretchen and Cleo and Annie, and the exuberant yapping of Gretchen's pups. Some of the older dogs were out in their run, and I slipped through the gate to join them. Two of them were so busy playing tug-of-war with a rubber ring that they hardly noticed me. But Sasha, the golden brown female with the right ear that never stood up straight, pranced over with a ball in her mouth, asking me to toss it for her.

"Oh, you're home," Mom said, coming out of the kennel with an empty feed pail. "How was school?"

I drew back my arm and sent the ball sailing toward the fence. "I miss Millbrook Elementary," I said, as Sasha skidded away. "I wish I could time-travel back a year."

"You'll get used to it," Mom said. "In a couple of weeks it'll all be old hat."

She set down the pail with a clatter and wiped her hands on her apron. "Listen, I've got to go pick up Melissa — she's having her hair done. And there's a family from Newton dropping by sometime this afternoon to look over Gretchen's litter. Show them around if I'm not back, will you?"

"Okay," I said. "Only — those pups are so little yet, just six weeks old — "

"They won't be taking one today," Mom

promised. "They're only looking."

"I know," I said. "Still, I hate to break up the gang. I never like to see them going one by one."

"You can't get attached to them all," Mom reminded me. "If we kept every pup they'd eat us into the poorhouse."

Sasha galloped back, tail wagging, and dropped the ball at my feet. "I wish somebody'd pick that one," Mom sighed. "She's no good for show with that ear, but she'd be a nice pet." After concentrating on show dogs all these years, breeding for perfect build and stance and gait, Mom didn't think much of dogs that were merely "pet quality." But there was something about Sasha that had always seemed special to me. I'd make sure the people from Newton didn't notice her.

After Mom left, I went into the kennel. I walked down the corridor past the kitchen and the bath area, past the cages of dogs we boarded for people on vacation, to the puppy room. The moment I opened the wire mesh door, wriggling bodies swirled around my feet. I squatted down, murmuring all the silly, nonsense things you can't help saying to puppies, stroking a head here, a squirming back there. Their teeth were needle sharp, but their fur still had that puppy fluffiness I loved.

The dark one with the white feet, that Mom had christened Hansel, tugged at my shoelace until it came undone. I scooped him onto my lap and he nibbled at my fingers. The kennel and the run were his entire world, safe and familiar. He couldn't guess that at any moment a stranger might snatch him away into an unknown future. Without warning or explanation he would have a new home, a new name, a new life.

Hansel clambered down to chase his brother's wiggling tail. I remember thinking that dogs were lucky. They lived in the present, bounding from moment to moment with never a worry about what lay ahead. I watched the frolicking pups with a real pang of envy. Looking back now, I wonder if that afternoon brought me the first inkling of the fears and uncertainties that loomed ahead for me.

Chapter 2

"Line up in your squads, girls! Nice and straight now — heads up, shoulders back!"

After nearly four weeks of school, we were used to the routine in phys ed class. Obediently we fell into our lines. I took my place in front of Brenda at the head of Squad Three. Ms. Corona crossed the gym, inspecting us all for flaws. Nancy Marasek had on blue socks instead of white ones, and Sheila McGraw's gym suit had a big tear in front, which she had tried to mend with a safety pin. Ms. Corona duly noted all such mortal sins in her marking book.

I sucked in my stomach and tried to stand ramrod straight. Ms. Corona's glance flicked harmlessly past me and she was on to Squad Four. "At ease," Brenda whispered, and we both giggled.

"Volleyball today," Ms. Corona shouted

cheerfully. "We'll divide the gym for two games. I need a couple of volunteers to set up the net."

I trailed after Nancy Marasek and two or three of the other girls who headed for the supply room. As we dragged out the nets and unearthed the volleyballs from behind the rolled-up tumbling mats, I remembered Dad's comment this morning at breakfast, that our school was known for its girls' athletics program, and that maybe I ought to go out for a sport this year. I did like to play games, though up to now my efforts at hitting a baseball or shooting a basket had been pretty substandard. Still, Dad seemed to hint, some day my hidden talent might yet burst forth.

Ms. Corona rolled a partition across the room, cutting it into two playing areas. I found myself on a team of seven, lined up between Nancy and Brenda. "We don't stand a chance," Nancy muttered. "Why did she give us Sheila McGraw? She's a world-class klutz!"

Before I could answer, the blast of the whistle ripped the air, and the game was on. Poised on my toes, I twisted this way and that to keep my eyes on the flying ball. It was everywhere at once, moving so fast it kept escaping from view. Then, for one dazzling instant, it hung directly before my face. I sprang forward and struck with both hands. The ball sailed back over the net and hit the floor with a glorious bounce.

"Way to go!" yelled Brenda. "We scored the first point!"

The room was a blur of motion, and the excitement of the game swept me along. Our whole team cheered each time we scored a point, and groaned when we missed a chance. Once more the ball plummeted toward me, and again I hurled it deftly back.

Maybe Dad was right. Maybe I should try out for the volleyball team. I'd compete against other schools all over North Jersey. I would develop breathtaking grace and awesome speed, and whenever I scored a point a cheer would rise from the bleachers. . . .

"Tracy!" Nancy cried. I snapped back to attention. Following her frantic gesture, I leaped almost in time. The ball skimmed off my fingertips and plopped to the floor behind me.

"They tied it up!" Brenda wailed. "Come on, we gotta make it!"

I wouldn't let my mind wander again, not for a fraction of a second! If we scored one more point, the game was ours. But the ball spun about so fast!

A burst of shouts made me turn to the end of the line in time to see Joyce Little spike the ball our way over the net. But Sue Rush on our team caught it before it touched the ground and sent it hurtling back. Then it vanished again amid the haze of whirling arms and legs.

"Tracy! Watch out!" Brenda screamed. I turned to look at her, but there was no sign of the ball. I whirled around, arms outstretched, and glimpsed it just as it plunged past my right shoulder to the floor. On the other side of the net, a joyful cheer rose up. It was almost loud enough to drown out the groans of disgust that surrounded me.

"You had to be *trying* to miss that one!" Nancy exclaimed. "It was right next to you!"

"Yeah, some people!" Sue Rush put in with a sneer. "Maybe you better get glasses."

"Come on, anybody can miss a ball once in a while," Brenda said. I threw her a grateful smile, but her words weren't quite convincing.

In the locker room I sank onto a bench in the corner. It was only a game, I told myself. Anybody could make a mistake. But I was the one who blew it, not Sheila the superklutz. The groan of my teammates echoed in my ears. Where had that ball come from? I'd been looking so hard, but I hadn't seen it until it was too late.

I'd never make the volleyball team, that was certain. Not even Ms. Corona could salvage me for the thrilling world of athletics.

The bell rang as I was tugging a comb through my rumpled hair, and I hurried out into the hall to dash for my next class. I didn't get lost much anymore, but I still hated the buffeting crowd. As I rounded the corner by Mrs. Blanchard's room, some guy slammed right into me and almost knocked me down before I saw him coming. My books tumbled to the floor, and he didn't even say he was sorry. Somebody else stepped on my hand as I crouched to pick them up.

"Hi, Tracy," said a girl's voice as I got to my feet. It came from somewhere off to the left, but for a second or two I couldn't figure out who had spoken. I stood brushing the dust from my hands, searching the throng, and finally focused in on a girl about my own height who seemed to be looking at me. I studied her long hair, print blouse, and round, smiling face, but she was only vaguely familiar.

"What's the matter? Don't you recognize me?" she demanded. "It's Joanne. I sit across from you in homeroom every morning!"

"Oh, I'm sorry! I didn't — I just — sure, Joanne! Hi!"

Embarrassment tangled my tongue around the words, and a hot flush crept up my cheeks. What was wrong with me? She remembered who I was, but hers was just one more face in the muddle of strangers' faces I encountered every day.

No wonder I despised Millbrook High, I thought, banging my books down onto my desk. There were just too many people. Most of them were rude, and even the nice ones came at you so fast you couldn't tell them apart.

And then there were all the boring classes. Mrs. Blanchard's English class, the last period in the day, felt like it would never end. The room was in the old part of the building, with ancient desks and chairs bolted to the floor, and such rotten lighting it was hard to read a book right in front of you. And Mrs. Blanchard droned on and on and on.

Today we were "building vocabulary," as she put it in her prim, polite way. She covered the front blackboard with words, and called on us one by one to go up and write the definitions. I tried to listen enough to know when my name would come up, while my mind wandered. I thought about Gretchen's litter, down to only two pups now. And Sasha, who was still unclaimed because nobody wanted a shepherd with a drooping right ear. Mom said she had a bad gene that hadn't surfaced in our stock for five generations —

"Tracy?"

I jumped. Mrs. Blanchard looked at me, waiting. I gazed at the columns sprawling across the board. I had no idea who had answered last or what word we had reached.

"You weren't listening," Mrs. Blanchard said sternly. "Come up and write a definition of the word *impending*."

Shakily I rose and started toward the front of the room. Impending . . . impending . . . the word spun through my brain. I'd looked it up last night, but now I couldn't remember what it meant. I stared at the blackboard, but I couldn't even see where the word was written.

The next thing I saw was the floor rushing up to meet me. A titter of laughter rippled through the room as I toppled forward. I clawed for balance at the rim of a desk, but momentum was against me. Without a shred of dignity, I pitched to my knees.

The laughter rose, then ebbed away as Mrs. Blanchard exclaimed, "Tracy, what happened? Are you all right?"

"I'm fine!" I gasped. I scrambled up, red-faced and shaken. At my feet lay the culprit — someone's bulky leather pocketbook. I had knocked it over and lipsticks, Kleenex, and change spilled across the floor.

"I'm sorry," I chattered. "I guess I wasn't looking. I just didn't see — "

"Never mind," Mrs. Blanchard said. "As long as you're in one piece. Now, please come up and define *impending* for us."

Somehow I reached the blackboard and stood, baffled, my mind a blank. "Impending," I repeated foolishly. "Impending means — um — it means — "

"Did you look up the words you were assigned last night?" There was no hint of politeness in Mrs. Blanchard's voice this time.

"I did," I stammered. "Only I forget what that one means." From the back of the room, one of the boys guffawed.

"*Impending*," Mrs. Blanchard informed me, "means 'forthcoming' or 'about to happen', usually in an ominous sense. Write the definition beside the word *impending* on the blackboard."

Frantically I scanned the columns of words before me. *Impending* was not among them. Slow, merciless seconds ticked by as I searched, but it simply wasn't there.

"Tracy, you're on the wrong side." Mrs. Blanchard picked up the pointer and tapped the board over to my left. Sure enough, the word glared out at me in bold white chalk. "About to happen, something ominous," I wrote, and fled back to my desk.

The instant the bell rang I dashed for the door, but I couldn't escape fast enough.

"Tracy," Mrs. Blanchard said behind me. "I'd like to speak with you a minute."

She was frowning as I approached her desk. "You realize that you haven't been doing very well so far this semester," she began. "You don't seem to be applying yourself. If you would pay more attention, I know you could be an A student."

"I do pay attention," I protested. "I mean, I *try* to." I didn't stand much chance of convincing her, not after today's performance.

"You have the potential," Mrs. Blanchard went on. "If you buckle down and work, you can be a top student, just like Melissa. But you don't watch what I put on the blackboard, and you don't seem to follow in your book when we're doing class assignments. And you should take more time with your homework, be more careful."

"I'll try to do better," I promised. I'd agree to anything if she'd let me leave!

"All right," she said, sighing. "I don't want to have to speak to you again."

I had almost reached the hall, when she stopped me once more. "Wait a minute," she called. "Something just occurred to me. When was the last time you had your eyes checked?"

"My eyes?" I repeated. "I don't know. I think we all got tested back in seventh grade."

"That was two years ago," Mrs. Blanchard said, shaking her head. "I'm going to send the nurse a note. She can set up an examination. It could be that you just need glasses."

"Oh, no!" I cried. "Not glasses! I couldn't — I mean, I see fine, I don't need anything like that!"

"You probably don't," Mrs. Blanchard said. "But it wouldn't hurt to find out for sure."

It *would* hurt, I thought as I trudged home. My life was turning into a long series of disasters, and glasses would be the crowning catastrophe. I was unremarkable-looking now, but with glasses I would be out-and-out ugly. While everybody around me grew more attractive and graceful day by day, I'd be peering out at the world like Mr. Magoo.

Mrs. Blanchard didn't get flustered when anybody else daydreamed through class. But I was "another Newbury girl." I was supposed to be perfect, a Melissa clone. And because I wasn't, she thought my eyesight was to blame.

Still, Mrs. Blanchard wasn't the only person who thought I needed glasses. Sue Rush had said the same thing this afternoon, after I blew the volleyball game. The way I kept bumping into people and tripping over things, maybe it was true.

As always, the barking of the dogs greeted

me as I came up the road to our driveway. I stopped at the mailbox and collected a handful of magazines and advertisements before I headed up to the house. "Hey, Tracy!" a voice shouted behind me. "Wait up!"

Even before I caught sight of his tall, slender figure loping toward me, I recognized Craig Martin's voice. Craig lived right across the street. He was a year ahead of me in school, and Brenda called him the Mad Scientist because he was always peering at bugs and things under his microscope. But he was also a confirmed dog lover. Sometimes he dropped over after school to play with the puppies or help out around the kennel. The minute I saw him I began to feel better. "Hi!" I called. "Come on over!"

We paused by the run to say hello to Gretchen and Annie and a big black Lab named Wolf, who was boarding for a couple of weeks. Then Sasha bounded over, dragging an enormous stick. She dropped it in front of us and looked up as if she deserved a prize.

"Hello, Sasha!" Craig said, sticking his fingers through the fence to stroke her muzzle. "You're such a nice dog! And you're very smart, too!"

"She really is," I said. "Yesterday I was

throwing a ball for her and trying to teach her to fetch, and she got the hang of it right away."

"She's so alert," Craig said. "Doesn't miss a thing."

To prove it, Sasha cocked her head, gazing off toward the kennel. Her left ear pricked up straight, but the right one flopped comically forward.

A moment later, Mom emerged and hurried toward us. "Sasha," she announced, "you are down for a bath today."

"How come?" I asked, suddenly alert myself. Being just "pet quality," Sasha didn't get a lot of special attention unless something was up.

"There's a family coming this afternoon to look for an older dog," Mom explained. "They just bought a farmhouse with five acres and — "

"They wouldn't want Sasha!" I protested. "Let them take Georgie or Max or — "

"Sasha would be just right," Mom insisted. "She's friendly, she'd be great with children . . ." She trailed off, looking at me hard.

I was silent for a moment, gathering my forces. "Mom," I began, "remember a couple of months ago you said maybe sometime I could have my own pup to raise?"

A knowing little frown wrinkled Mom's forehead. She guessed what was coming.

"Instead of a puppy," I begged, "could I keep Sasha?"

"Wouldn't you rather have a dog you could raise from the time it's little?" Mom asked. "Sasha's a year old already."

"That's okay," I said. "She still *acts* like a puppy, that's for sure."

Mom wouldn't give up. "I thought you'd like a dog you could show in confirmation trials. You've always seemed interested. And Sasha — with that ear, she doesn't meet the shepherd standards. She wouldn't qualify to enter."

I was doing this all wrong. Mom was disappointed in my choice. How could I explain that spark I felt for Sasha, that sense that she was somehow special?

I glanced over at Craig in a wordless plea for help. "Looks don't count in obedience trials, do they?" he asked. "As long as it's a purebred dog?"

When Mom nodded, I rushed ahead, caught up in Craig's idea. "I'll enter her in obedience matches. I'll train her, take her to classes, it'll be really neat!"

"Well," Mom said, shaking her head, "it's up to you. I still think a puppy — but if you want to keep Sasha — "

"I do! I really do!" I cried.

"Well then, I guess she's yours."

"Hurray!" Craig and I shouted together. I ran to the gate and let Sasha out of the run. Wild with excitement, she raced from me to Craig to Mom, flinging herself on each of us in turn. But in the end, when she flopped down in panting exhaustion, she curled up at my feet. She didn't have to be told twice that she was my dog now.

Chapter 3

For two days I let myself hope that Mrs. Blanchard had forgotten our talk after class. Then, in homeroom Friday morning, I found a grim summons from the school nurse waiting on my desk.

Miss Mendoza was better known as Miss Band-Aid, because that's about the only thing she ever prescribed. But she did have an eye chart in her office. She rolled it down and asked me to read the nonsense strings of letters. I thought I did fine, but she still frowned and said that I ought to see an optometrist for a routine examination, just to be on the safe side.

The optometrist, Dr. Abramowitz, had even more complicated charts in his office. He kept telling me not to be so nervous, and not to turn my head this way and that all the time. I didn't know how he thought I could see all those letters *without* turning my head. But I figured it was safer to keep my mouth shut, not to raise any unnecessary questions.

As it turned out, keeping my mouth shut didn't help. When the examination was over he called Mom in from the waiting room and told us that there was nothing seriously wrong. However, I might be able to see the blackboard at school more easily with some slight correction. Correction meant glasses.

My prescription, Dr. Abramowitz explained, would be ready on Saturday, in just four days. Four precious days of freedom. "I feel like a suspect condemned to the gallows," I told Brenda on the phone that night.

"Guys don't make passes at girls who wear glasses," she teased.

"Thanks a lot," I said. "You sure know how to make me feel better."

"It might not be too bad," she tried to console me. "Maybe you can just use them for reading. Nobody will have to see you wear them that much."

"I'm supposed to wear them all the time," I said gloomily. "All the time and everywhere." Brenda could only groan in sympathy.

"The main thing is for you to see better," Mom said firmly as we climbed out of the car.

"That's what really counts, isn't it?"

Was it? I wondered. The brand-new glasses straddling my face declared to the world that I was defective. Maybe I was, but I didn't have to advertise it. "They don't make things look any clearer yet," I said. "I'd probably see better without them."

"You heard what the doctor said," Mom reminded me. "You'll get used to them in a week or so if you wear them every day. And eventually you can try contact lenses."

"Eventually," I repeated dismally. "That could be months!"

She started up the driveway, and turned back to study me from a little distance. "I think they're rather becoming on you," she stated. "They make you look older, you know that?"

"Great!" I muttered. "They can start calling me Granny!"

"I give up!" Mom exclaimed. "You may look older, but you sure aren't acting very grown-up about this!"

I knew she was right, but I didn't care. I stamped into the house and glared at myself in the vestibule mirror. My hair was rumpled, my complexion was blotchy, and the glasses presided over it all. "Grotesque," I said out loud. Sometimes those words from Mrs. Blanchard's vocabulary lists fit just right.

"What's the matter?" Melissa asked, coming up behind me.

"What do you think's the matter?" I snapped. I turned around to let her get the full face-to-face view.

"I think," she said, in that slow, measured way she had, as though she was about to utter something truly profound, "that it's no big deal."

"You're not the one who's got to wear them," I pointed out. "You lead a charmed life. Anybody could tell just by looking at you, you're not the type who would ever need glasses."

Before she could reply, I marched upstairs and flung myself across my bed. Down in the living room Mom switched on the vacuum cleaner, as if to remind me that life went on. I wondered what Brenda would say when she saw the glasses on me? Would Sue Rush gloat and say, "I told you so"?

Above the vacuum's steady whine I became aware of a faint scratching sound. I slid off the bed and opened the door. Sasha burst inside as though she'd been fired from a cannon. She leaped up on me with all four paws and tried to lick my face.

"Down, girl! Down!" I cried. I pushed her to the floor, and she raced around me in circles, her whole body wriggling with joy.

"Come on, you act as if I'd been gone a year," I protested. At the sound of my voice she made another try for my face, knocking my glasses askew. She didn't seem to notice them at all.

It's hard to stay depressed after a greeting like that. Sasha unearthed her nylon bone from under the bed, and after we played a brisk game of tug-of-war, life seemed a lot less bleak. I even found myself wondering if the glasses might, after all, help me read faster. It would be nice not to spend so many hours hunched over my homework every night.

I picked up my social studies book and flipped to tonight's assignment. The letters loomed unnaturally large, and they were fuzzy around the edges. Maybe Mom was right, and I'd adjust to this new way of seeing the world. From the way things looked today, though, I had my doubts.

Sasha bounded to the door and turned to look at me with an expectant cock of the head. She was right. It was silly to sit in my room feeling sorry for myself. Afternoon sunlight slanted through the window. A bit of the day still survived, enough time for us both to enjoy a walk.

For a moment I considered leaving my glasses on the night table. Mom was so busy she might not even notice if I slipped out without them. But Melissa would be sure to comment if she saw me. There was no way around it. I was doomed to wear them from now on.

As I followed Sasha downstairs, I felt a twinge of shame over the obnoxious way I'd been acting. To my relief, I didn't meet anyone as I took Sasha's leash from the hook in the kitchen and let myself out the back door, to the usual clamor of barking dogs.

Sasha had experienced many changes in her life since she became my dog, moving from the kennel into the house. She had to get used to vacuum cleaners and doorbells and telephones, and to learn all sorts of rules about staying off the furniture and not chewing up socks. She still found her leash an object of mystery. As soon as I snapped it to her collar she rolled onto her back and tried to bite it, as if it were some odd new toy.

"Come on," I said, giving the leash a gentle tug. "Get up. Let's go see Craig."

Sasha never did anything the easy way. Instead of simply standing up, she turned a funny little half-somersault that landed her on her feet. She stood still, legs splayed, gazing over her shoulder toward the kennel.

"You don't live there any more," I reminded her. "You've moved up in the world."

I tugged again, and this time she bounded ahead as far as she could, stretching the leash taut. "Sasha, heel!" I said, pulling her back with a quick jerk. I tried to sound as commanding as Mom did when she trained dogs, but the message didn't get through. Sasha lunged forward again. Her breath rasped as she strained against the collar.

Stopping and starting, we made slow progress down the driveway. Finally, as we turned to walk along the road, Sasha gave up the fight. Tilting back her ears resignedly, she trotted by my left side as though she had been heeling all her life.

"Good girl!" I exclaimed. "What a good dog, Sasha!" The sound of praise broke the spell. Overjoyed, Sasha leaped up on me, wagging her tail and playfully nipping my hand.

We found Craig in his laboratory — the old toolshed where he did all of his scientific experiments and observations. I hesitated in the doorway, bracing myself for his reaction when he saw my glasses. He'd be too polite to say how awful I looked, but I'd know what he really thought.

Craig was so intent on gazing through his microscope that at first he didn't even notice us. I stepped cautiously inside. It was no wonder kids called him the Mad Scientist. The shed was a jumble of jars and bottles and stacks of books. In its cage in the corner, a white mouse raced endlessly in its exercise wheel. On a plank table lay the treasure Craig had found in the woods last week — the partially assembled skeleton of a possum.

Sasha's nose quivered with excitement at the dazzling new smells. I wound her leash tightly around my hand to keep her from wandering into trouble. "Craig?" I called softly.

"Tracy!" he exclaimed. "Hi! I was just looking at this feather. It's incredible! You'd never think it was so complex, just seeing it with the naked eye, you know?"

"Can I see?" I asked with interest. Keeping Sasha on a tight rein, I approached the table and peered through the lens. A great, shifting blur swam across the glass. It didn't look like a feather, or even a section of a feather. It didn't look like anything I could describe.

"What's the matter?" Craig asked at my shoulder.

"Nothing," I said. "I guess it's these darn glasses, they make things look weird!"

"Oh, hey," Craig said. "I didn't even notice." He was no more impressed by my glasses than Sasha was.

I snatched them off and stared into the microscope again. I saw only the same immense, viscous mass. "I guess you have to be used to looking through this thing," I said, shaking my head. "I can't figure it out."

"Let me adjust the — " Craig began, when there was a crash of splintering glass. Trembling, Sasha threw herself against my legs. A cloud of choking chemical fumes filled the room.

"Sasha!" I cried, reeling back. "What did you do?"

"It's okay," Craig said, stooping to inspect the mess. "She knocked over a jar of formaldehyde. Probably hit it with her tail."

"I'm sorry," I told him. "I should have kept my eye on her." I scooped Sasha into my arms, safely away from the splinters of glass, and carried her outside. I tied her to a fence post where, I hoped, she couldn't do any more mischief. Then I plunged back inside to help Craig mop up.

"I shouldn't have brought her in here," I said apologetically. "This is definitely not a dog place."

Craig didn't argue. I followed him outside and we leaned against the fence, drawing delicious lungfuls of fresh air. Sasha lay on her stomach, her tail twitching hopefully, waiting for our forgiveness.

"Well, hello, Sasha," Craig said, going over to her and bending to offer a pat. "I didn't even greet you properly yet."

Sasha jumped up and lapped his face with

her long pink tongue. "Okay, okay!" Craig gasped, laughing. "Cool it, will you?"

"Sasha, cut it out!" I exclaimed. "Sit!"

To my astonishment, Sasha folded her hind legs and sat, ears erect, tail thumping. She looked from me to Craig and back to me again.

"I don't believe it!" I cried. "She didn't do that, did she?"

"Come on, give her some credit," Craig protested. "She sat."

"Good girl, Sasha!" I cried. In a flash she was on her feet again, prancing to the end of the leash in her effort to reach me.

"It was pure chance," I said. "I've hardly tried to teach her anything. She couldn't begin to know what 'sit' means."

"Well, I always figured she's smart," Craig said. "She picks things up before you know it!"

"Why doesn't she learn to quit chewing up shoes, then?" I asked. I pointed to the mangled toe of my right sneaker.

"Oh, that's too boring," Craig said, grinning. "She's interested in higher things, right, pup? You're going to be a first-class obedience champ, aren't you?"

"She likes socks, too," I said. "And living room drapes. Even Melissa's favorite cashmere sweater."

"You see? She's got good taste."

"Good taste, all right," I giggled. "To her everything tastes good."

"I mean it, though," Craig said, sitting back on his heels. "When are you going to start her in an obedience class? You told your mother you wanted to."

"Actually, I got the name of a lady that runs a class like that Saturday mornings," I told him. "I'm going to start taking her next week."

"You probably know a lot more about training than you realize," Craig said. "Don't forget, you already taught her to sit just by accident."

"It was an accident, all right," I said. "Sit, Sasha! Sit!"

This time, as I expected, Sasha completely ignored me. She pounced on a stick and wrestled it between her front paws.

"Nobody's perfect," Craig said. "She'll get it down pretty soon. Listen, do you think I could help you train her? We could get some books and work together, on top of what you do in your class."

"Sure," I said. "That'd be fun. Besides, I can use all the help I can get."

As we sat there on the grass, Craig and Sasha seemed to be receding from me, slipping gradually into shadow. I fumbled in my pocket and put my glasses back on. For a few moments the yard and the fence and the laboratory shed swelled large into my view. But perhaps it was only my imagination. Darkness was setting in.

"I forgot it's so late," I said. "I guess I better be getting home."

Naturally Craig had a scientific explanation. "Daylight Savings Time is over now. It gets dark an hour earlier than we're used to."

I stood up and unhitched Sasha from the fence. Straining my eyes, I could barely make out the edge of the green lawn and the swath of blackness beyond, which had to be the road. "See you," I told Craig, and started across the grass.

"See you," Craig echoed behind me. I could barely see his upraised arm as he waved good-bye.

Up ahead a car swept into view, and for an instant the road shone clearly in the glare of headlights. Then the car was gone, and the darkness folded around me again. I walked on, testing the ground with my feet at each step, until the soft grass changed abruptly to hard, flat asphalt.

What was the matter with me? I must have walked back and forth from our house to Craig's at night a hundred times before. I couldn't remember that it was ever especially difficult or scary. But tonight the darkness was deeper somehow, as though all of my familiar landmarks were buried in fog.

"Craig!" I called. He didn't answer. He was probably busy in the lab again, too absorbed to hear me. Anyway, he'd think I was crazy if I asked him to walk me home. Maybe Mom would come out looking for me, or Melissa. But no one had seen me leave the house. As far as they knew, I was still up in my room, feeling sorry for myself. They would probably decide to leave me sulking there until I was ready to come down on my own.

In my hand I still clutched Sasha's leash. Now she tugged sharply to the left, jarring me to action. All I had to do, I realized, was turn left and follow the grassy shoulder of the road. I could just make out the patch of ground at my feet, the ragged line of green that bordered the darker pavement. By keeping my left foot on the grass I knew I wouldn't wander into the middle of the road unaware.

Sasha tugged insistently, frustrated by my slow, tentative pace. This time I didn't attempt to make her heel. She seemed to know exactly where she wanted to go, and I was happy to follow her. Perhaps, like a milkman's horse, she knew the homeward route.

We passed a patch of glimmering lights,

which had to be the Worthingtons' place, and I followed the curve of the road around to the right. I wasn't lost. I couldn't get lost on Hickory Road.

Then, up ahead, I heard the wild barking of the dogs. Sasha surged toward the sound, and I scrambled after her in a desperate half-run. I stumbled over the row of stones that edged the driveway just as a light flashed on and the house sprang into focus, solid and real and safe. I was home.

"Tracy!" Mom called from the back door. "I was just going to call Brenda's mother to see if you were over there. We're sitting down to dinner. Melissa's got a date tonight, so we're eating a little early."

"These glasses were a gigantic waste of money," I said, clattering up the back steps. "They don't help me see any better at all."

"Will you just give them time?" Mom exclaimed, tossing her hands in the air. "And watch Sasha's feet, I just did the floor! Where in the world *were* you, anyway?"

"I was at Craig's," I said. I crouched to wipe Sasha's muddy paws. My knees were trembling. I wasn't sure if it was from relief at being home safe, or from fear. Fear of something . . . something impending.

Chapter 4

Six o'clock already! I'd promised Brenda I'd be at her house by seven, a little early to help her set up before the other guests arrived. I finished sorting through my records and piled a stack of albums and cassettes on the love seat by the front door, where I couldn't forget them. And there were still more things to do.

Sasha scampered at my heels as I dashed upstairs to wrap Brenda's birthday present, a beautiful red mohair scarf. I ran my hands over its silky softness as it lay across my lap, and caught myself wishing I didn't have to give it away.

As I began to unroll the wrapping paper, Sasha leaped onto the bed to get a closer look. Playfully she pounced on the roll and tried to push it to the floor.

"Sasha, no!" I shouted. I shoved her off the

bed and she crouched in shame, her ears back, tail between her legs.

"Oh, come on, I'm not that mad," I said. "Just don't rip the paper up, that's all."

Sasha brightened. Her tail twitched, and her left ear pricked up while the right one flopped comically. She stared at me, poised to spring onto the bed again.

"Stay," I commanded. Sasha heaved a resigned sigh and settled her muzzle onto her outstretched paws until I finished my gift-wrapping.

"Okay, come on," I said, when I had signed Brenda's card. "Now you've got to work."

I took Sasha's leash from the doorknob, and she bounded after me down the stairs. In the living room, where there was plenty of space, I snapped the leash to her collar, stepped away from her, and commanded, "Sasha, come."

Sasha pranced forward and paused in front of me, waiting. She was a step or two farther away than she should be, according to Mrs. Barton, who taught our obedience class Saturday mornings. But she was definitely getting the idea.

"Sasha, heel," I ordered, giving the leash a little tug. Passing it from one hand to the other, I brought her around behind me to my left side. "Sasha, sit," I told her firmly. But she stood motionless until I bent and pressed her rump to the floor with an encouraging, "Good girl!" For a fleeting moment we resembled the picture in the obedience manual — the dog at sit, straight and alert at the handler's left heel.

Then Melissa breezed in, and Sasha burst into action, straining at the end of the leash to greet her. "What're you doing?" Melissa inquired on her way across the room.

"Nothing much," I said. "Just trying to do some obedience exercises."

"Oh yeah?" Melissa paused in the kitchen doorway. "How's she doing?"

Melissa was never very interested in the dogs. They annoyed her when they jumped up and spattered her with muddy footprints, or when their hair clung to her otherwise spotless clothes. Sometimes she grumbled that the yapping from the kennel was going to drive her crazy. So I didn't really expect her to give Sasha's obedience training more than a passing nod.

"Oh, she's doing just great, can't you tell?" I said, as Sasha made another leap. "Look at her grace, her style!"

"What are you trying to teach her?" Melissa asked, backing away.

"Well, there's a set bunch of things you teach them for novice trials. Come and sit, down, stay, heel, stuff like that. Nothing all that exciting."

Melissa disappeared and I put Sasha through the come-and-sit routine two or three more times. I was about to try down-and-stay when Melissa returned with a handful of celery sticks. She had some personal rule against snacks that taste good.

"Can I watch?" she asked.

"If you want," I said, surprised. I hesitated, half expecting her to change her mind, but she stood there looking at me. "Sasha, down!" I said, with a downward tug on the leash. For a second or two she braced her legs, stiff as posts. Then, inch by tortured inch, she sank to the carpet.

"Good girl," I said. Mrs. Barton said you always have to praise your dog for making the attempt, to give them the right idea.

I turned to Melissa apologetically. "That's not exactly how she's supposed to do it, but at least she's down, right?"

"Wrong," Melissa said, laughing. I glanced back just in time to see Sasha bounce to her feet with a mischievous wag of her tail.

"You hopeless mutt!" I exclaimed. "I think we're going to quit for today. Stay tuned tomorrow."

"I don't know how you stick with it," Melissa

said. "You've got more patience than I do."

"Me!" I exclaimed. "You've got to be kidding!"

She was the one with the patience, I thought, as I slipped on the new top I was wearing to Brenda's party. I worked with Sasha for half an hour, while Melissa practiced the violin dutifully four hours every day.

Even though my arms were loaded with records, I managed to carry a flashlight as I walked to Brenda's house. For all the years we had been friends, I'd almost never bothered taking the long way around by the road. But tonight I didn't dare take the shortcut through the woods. At half-past six it was already pitch dark out, and the comforting beam of my flashlight barely showed me the patch of road in front of my feet.

For the hundredth time in the past three weeks, ever since the day I got my glasses, I tried to remember other walks at night. I never minded taking the shortcut to Brenda's after supper last summer, but in July and August it stayed light until eight or eight-thirty. This time last year — early November — were the nights ever this dark? Was it so hard to see where to put down my feet?

Nobody liked walking around at night, I

tried to assure myself. That's why they invented flashlights. Probably I had always felt this way about dark hallways and unlighted stretches along the road. I just hadn't thought about it much before, so I couldn't quite remember.

I had to admit that no one seemed to notice my glasses very much. The trouble was that they didn't help me see any better than I could before. At first when I complained, Mom insisted that it was "all in my head," that I was just making excuses not to wear them. Finally she said maybe we should go back to Dr. Abramowitz and get thicker lenses. After that I wore the glasses faithfully every day, and didn't complain anymore.

The front porch light cast a welcoming glow as I rounded the corner, and Brenda opened the door before I had time to ring the bell.

"Come on!" she exclaimed. "You've got to see my birthday present! And *hear* it, that's the main thing."

Brenda raced ahead of me and pounded down the stairs to the basement. I hesitated at the top, gazing down into a well of gloom. "Hey, could you turn on some more light down there?" I called.

Brenda's voice floated up out of the abyss. "Yeah, sure. How's this?" A switch clicked, and the stairs wavered into view. I still felt a bit uncertain as I started down, as though I were making my way through a thin, rippling mist.

In the basement rec room, the mist cleared enough to let me take a good look at the couch and the scattered folding chairs, the card tables covered with crepe paper, and the only feature that really mattered — Brenda's brand-new birthday stereo system. "See, here's the turntable and the cassette deck, and down here's the CD player," Brenda said proudly. "Oh yeah, and there are the headsets. Mom insisted on those — but tonight's special, seeing as it is the only birthday party I'm likely to have all year."

I dumped my pile of albums onto the stack in the cabinet. Brenda put on something by Cyndi Lauper, and we curled up on the couch to listen. The sound was exquisite, from the power of the throbbing bass and the quivering, electronic strings, to the vibrant voice shining over it all.

"Wow!" I said when the first cut was over. "I wonder if I can talk my folks into getting me a system like this sometime!"

"Christmas?" Brenda suggested.

I shook my head. "I got my Christmas present already. Sasha. And I won't be fifteen till August."

48

"Well, you can just hang out here a lot," Brenda said. "We can share." She jumped up. "We better put out the refreshments! What if this party turns out to be a complete bust?"

"Don't worry," I told her. "It'll be perfect."

We had just filled the bowls with potato chips and pretzels when the first guests arrived. I knew Nancy Marasek from p.e. class, but I had never met her date before — a tall, scrawny guy with flaming red hair who said his name was Dan. Nancy began a complicated story about how she almost hadn't been allowed to come after the fight she'd had with her mother that afternoon over cleaning her room. Before she had time to finish, more people came clumping down the stairs. Stephanie and Jamie had been two of my best friends in grammar school, and it felt like a reunion when they walked in. The noise level rose as more boys arrived. A couple of them belonged to the old grammar school gang, too, but three or four more were total strangers. I glimpsed Craig over by the refreshment table, but I could hardly reach him through the crowd.

Brenda stood on the bottom step and gazed out over the room, counting heads. "Eighteen . . . twenty . . . twenty-three . . . oh, I missed him — that's twenty-four!" She almost danced with excitement. "This'll be the biggest, best party ever!"

"Hey guys!" Nancy called. "Let's dance!" In moments we were dragging chairs to the side of the room, clearing a dance floor. At first we all stood back on the fringes, surveying the suddenly empty space a little skeptically. Then Nancy and Dan marched boldly into the center and began to sway and swing with the music. A burly, blond boy in a blue T-shirt said something to Brenda, and she followed him, grinning, to join Nancy and Dan.

Someone touched my shoulder. I turned to see Craig, smiling and holding out his hand. "Tracy, you want to dance?" he asked.

"Sure." The floor was filling up already, but we claimed a corner under the left speaker for our own. I struggled to keep Craig's arms and hands in view as he moved to the quick, pulsing beat.

"I didn't know you were into fast dancing," I told him. "I can hardly keep up with you."

Craig chuckled. "Us mad scientists, we've got lots of hidden talents."

Dan stepped to the stereo as the song faded out, and cranked up the volume. With a roar of drums like cannonfire, the next cut rocked the room. Craig said something, but his words were lost beneath the pounding of the music.

Conversation was no longer an issue. It was time to clear the clutter of words from my head, to give myself wholly to dancing. Suddenly I knew that I didn't have to mirror the flickering movements of Craig's hands and the precise way his body wove to the bass line. I found my own rhythm in the music, and I knew that however I danced would be fine.

People began to press into our private corner, gradually drawing Craig and me out toward the center. In the swirl of people, someone stepped into the space between us, and I faced a pudgy, round-cheeked boy with a toothy smile. I smiled back and kept on dancing.

"Now we're really rolling!" Brenda exclaimed in the next lull between songs.

"This is how a party's supposed to be!" I said, beaming at her. "I told you it'd be just perfect!"

And it would have been perfect, too, if someone hadn't dimmed the lights.

I don't know whose idea it was. Suddenly, as the next cut thundered in around us, the room sank into darkness. In an instant the swaying dancers disappeared, the chairs and tables vanished, and the room itself lost all dimensions. In a spasm of horror I imagined a vast pit cracking wide before my feet. If I moved, if I took a single step, I would plunge down and down and be swallowed in darkness forever.

"Turn the lights back on!" My voice shrilled high and frantic over the opening chords of the next song.

"Come off it!" one of the boys protested. "Don't ruin the mood!"

Beside me a girl's voice murmured in agreement. With a jolt I realized that the others enjoyed the hovering gloom. For them it transformed the ordinary basement rec room into a place deliciously mysterious, full of secret nooks and private corners. No one else pleaded for light. I was utterly alone.

Thudding drums and the scream of electric guitars crashed across the brief piano interlude. It was no longer music to sweep me into the dance. The suffocating cloud of sound choked off the voices around me and made my isolation complete. I stood frozen, afraid to move in any direction, while my heart raced on a rising crest of panic.

A hand touched my arm, and a boy's voice shouted something I couldn't understand. It had to be my partner, the boy with the toothy grin, wondering why I'd stopped dancing. I tried to force my arms and legs back into the rhythm that had come so naturally a few minutes ago, but my limbs had grown stiff. "I don't feel like it right now," I shouted, hoping he could read my lips. He certainly couldn't have heard me.

People would wonder what was wrong with me if I stood planted to this spot much longer. I pictured the buzz of questions, the concerned hands reaching to take charge of me. The thought of that was even more terrifying than the darkness.

Breathe deep, I told myself sternly. This is Brenda's basement, where you've been a hundred times! There aren't any pits in the floor, there are no monsters out to get you! Just don't lose your cool, and you'll be all right!

My panic subsided a little, and I fought my way toward a plan. I would find the edge of the room. Once I discovered the wall, perhaps I could figure out where I was. At least I could stay still in a safe place and hope that no one noticed me.

Slowly, cautiously, I inched forward. With each step my foot tested the floor to be sure that it was solid beneath me. Maybe in the gloom no one would see the way I stretched my hands ahead of me to fend off obstacles. The picture of an octopus flashed into my mind, something I'd seen last week on a TV special. When it didn't want to be seen, it hid itself in a cloud of black ink. I was like the octopus, surrounded by a black cloud — but I couldn't see out, and the people around me could see in.

Once my shoulder collided with someone who grunted in surprise. "Sorry," I muttered, and tried to walk a little faster, but something hard caught me across the shins and I pitched forward onto a clattering pile of chairs just as the song faded to a shuddering silence.

A nebulous form materialized beside me, and Craig's voice demanded, "Tracy, are you okay?"

"Of course!" I snapped. My right shin was on fire, and I felt a warm trickle down my ankle which had to be blood. But I couldn't admit that I was hurt, it would unleash too many questions.

"You sure?" he persisted. "You look like — "

"I'm fine!" I repeated. "It just made a lot of noise, that's all. I can't help it if I'm a klutz."

"What'd you do, trip over the chairs?" Brenda demanded, hurrying over. "That's the only problem with the lighting down here, isn't it?"

I mustered a feeble laugh. "You could say so, yeah."

The cassette clicked off. Other voices

emerged and I began to place the people around me. The hiss of a flip-top can and the tinkle of ice told me that the refreshment table was a few yards to my right. That would mean that I wasn't far from the foot of the stairs.

"Did you bring that Whitney Houston album?" Brenda was saying. "I don't see it in the stack."

"I brought it," I said. "It's got to be there somewhere."

"Could you come look?" Brenda begged. "I really want to hear it."

Obediently I followed the wavering blur that was Brenda's back. "Here," she said in a moment. "Maybe you'll have better luck than I had."

"It'd help if we had a little more light," I said, but she didn't reply. I crouched down and flipped through the pile of albums, pretending to search. Even when I bent close, I couldn't make out any of their covers.

"You're looking for Whitney Houston?" It was Craig again, somewhere off to my left. "It's right here, on top of the tape deck."

A hand floated before my face, and I reached up to take the record jacket.

"Oh, thanks," I said. He could have handed me "A Visit to Sesame Street," for all I knew.

"Hey, you're sure you didn't hurt yourself back there?" Craig pursued. "You really took a header, I saw you."

"You don't have to keep reminding me!" I shot back.

"Oh. I'm sorry. I didn't mean. . . ." Craig trailed off. Before I could apologize, he faded into the crowd again.

Brenda snatched the record from me, and I heard it flop onto the turntable. In another minute the room would drown in noise again. I couldn't bear it. If only they would turn the lights back on — but I didn't dare ask again.

"Brenda," I said, "I don't feel so good. I think I'd better go home."

"You can't!" she cried. "I mean, the party's just getting started — you can't leave already! Have some soda, that'll fix you right up."

"No thanks. I just better go." I pointed myself toward the place where the stairs ought to be, and tried to walk without shuffling my feet. It wasn't easy. At any minute I was sure to overturn a table.

"Hey, you don't look too good," Brenda said. She folded a steadying hand over my arm and I followed her gratefully. My toe struck something hard and hollow that had to be the bottom step. I found the banister as Brenda began to climb ahead of me. At the top she threw open the door into the brightly lit kitchen. I squinted against the dazzling stream of light. It was too much, more than I could bear, and I stumbled over the top step. For a few moments I couldn't see any better there than I could in the basement.

Dimly, Brenda's figure slid into focus. She stood by the table, a worried frown creasing her forehead. "You want to lie down?" she asked. "Maybe my mom can get you something."

My plan of action hadn't gone this far. As the kitchen cabinets and the sink and the gleaming stove took shape, I felt so relieved to see clearly that I couldn't think very clearly. "I'll call my folks," I said. "Somebody can pick me up."

Brenda hesitated. "Okay, if you really want to," she said, gesturing toward the phone on the wall. "Too bad you've got to miss the rest of the party."

I didn't have to lie to her. I'd explain that there was something really wrong with my eyes. I'd tell her how scared I was downstairs, how I couldn't walk around down there without making a fool of myself. She was my best friend. I could tell her anything. . . .

"Brenda? Where'd you go?" a boy's voice called from below.

Brenda's cheeks flushed with pleasure. She glanced at me apologetically. "I've got to go. That's David — the guy I was dancing with. You'll be all right? You're sure?"

"Sure, I'm sure." I tried to sound feeble enough to be convincingly sick, but not so weak that she'd get alarmed. She gave me a long parting look and hurried back downstairs.

As I dialed our number I considered the possibilities. When Mom or Dad or Melissa answered, I could have a headache, or cramps, or a touch of stomach flu. It was all right to have any of those ordinary ailments that struck you down for a little while and let you bounce back up again. But I was certain now that I had something that didn't just go away. There was something wrong with me that set me apart from everyone at the party, from all of the people I had ever known. Maybe I was going blind.

Chapter 5

Brenda was in love. She called me the morning after the party, so full of the news that I couldn't imagine breaking in with a downer like the problem with my eyes. It was David Cuyler, the big blond boy who asked her to dance right at the beginning. He was so cute, and had such a neat sense of humor, and he hardly danced with anybody else, and she couldn't stop thinking about him! She couldn't get him out of her mind for three straight seconds!

Monday after school she met me by my locker with the next chapter. "David and I both have fifth-period lunch!" she chattered. "I can't believe I never noticed him before! Today I got into line and I looked up, and there he was, about four people ahead of me. And he said, 'Brenda, come here!' This girl behind him gave me the dirtiest look but I didn't care, I cut right in front of her to stand with him!"

The burned-out bulbs in the hall had been replaced weeks ago, but the lighting in the basement was dim at best. Still, I didn't need to see Brenda's face to know she was beaming. "Did you sit together?" I asked, pulling my coat out of my locker.

"Yeah, and then we went out on the lawn till the bell rang. It was freezing out there, and we had the whole place practically to ourselves. We had to run around to keep warm. He grabbed my hand and we ran and ran like crazy!"

For a moment I let myself imagine it — how wonderful it would be to run and laugh with someone special, as if you were the only two people in the world. But pretty soon I might not be able to run without stumbling and sprawling, even in the open with the sun shining down. I shoved the thought of romance out of my mind and slammed my locker shut.

My spirits lifted once we got outside. After the first few moments, when the sudden glare blotted out everything around me, the world rose clear and bold and splendid. By the time we were halfway home I found myself wondering again if I might be wrong about my eyes after all. Maybe I did need stronger glasses, as Mom had suggested. Dr. Abramowitz would change my prescription, and I'd be able to joke about the time I actually thought I was going blind.

"You've got to meet David and tell me what you think," Brenda was saying. "You should have stayed the other night. You would have seen what he's like if you hadn't left the party so early." Maybe it was my imagination, but I thought her tone was more accusing than regretful.

"I would have loved to," I said. "Only — "

"I know, you couldn't help it," Brenda said. "Oh, no! Look who's coming!"

Sheila McGraw shambled toward us around the corner. She always looked haphazard, as though she'd been put together by accident. Today her ponytail was half undone and one shoelace straggled loose, but she managed not to trip as she hurried to meet us. "Hey, you guys!" she called. "Where you going?"

"Just home," Brenda said.

"I'll walk with you?" There was a question in Sheila's voice.

Brenda glanced at me with a shake of her head. But we couldn't exactly tell her no. "Sure," I said. "Might as well."

Somehow Brenda didn't want to talk about David with Sheila around, but he was the only thought in her head, so she had nothing else to say. "Um, what have you been doing lately?" I asked Sheila, to fill in the silence.

Sheila scuffed noisily through a patch of gravel. "Nothing much," she muttered. "I've got to go home and babysit my little brother."

"What a drag," I said.

The silence started stretching out again. It must be awful to sense that people groaned when they saw you coming, and tried to go the other way. What was it about Sheila that turned people off? Her clothes, or the way she never had anything much to say? Or was she just too smart in school?

"One thing, though," she said suddenly, as though she'd been rummaging her brain for a conversational tidbit, "one thing — I might go to Brussels this summer."

"You mean, where they have the sprouts?" Brenda giggled.

Sheila giggled faintly, not sure if Brenda were making fun of her. "It's in Belgium," she said. "I've got cousins that live over there. I'm trying to learn Flemish."

"Flemish?" Brenda repeated. "I never even heard of it." Her tone made it plain that if she had never heard of a thing, it couldn't be worth knowing.

"It's what they speak over there," Sheila said. "Well, see you guys later. 'Bye." She waved awkwardly, nearly losing her grip on her armload of books, and turned down her street.

"What in the world is she going to say in Flemish!" Brenda crowed as soon as Sheila was out of earshot. "She can hardly even talk in English!"

I forced a laugh, but it wasn't really that funny. For just a moment I felt that Brenda and I were very far apart, almost strangers.

"Come on in for a while," she said when we got to her house. "I've got some new tapes, or we can watch TV or something."

"Okay," I said, and followed her up the familiar front steps. She was herself again, Brenda Novak, my best friend since sixth grade.

Brenda's mom bought Cokes and potato chips by the case, so there was always a healthy supply of food around. We helped ourselves and settled down in the den to watch the tail end of *General Hospital*. "Do you think David'll call?" Brenda asked dreamily as the commercials came on.

"Has he got your number?" I asked.

"He wrote it inside the cover of his math book. But what if he doesn't have math homework tonight? My number'll be sitting there in his locker!"

"If he said he'll call, then he probably will," I pointed out.

She sighed and scooped up another handful of chips. "If he wants to, he will. But then if he doesn't call, that means he doesn't want to! I'll die!"

"How come you're dying all of a sudden? A couple of minutes ago you were *ecstatic*." Sometimes Mrs. Blanchard's vocabulary words popped out when I didn't even know they were coming.

Brenda gave me a playful kick. "You know what I mean! I *am* — whatever you said. And I will *die* if he forgets his math book!"

In what must have been the fifth commercial, two mothers discussed a miracle cure for diaper rash. Then came a toothpaste ad and a thirty-second news bulletin and a spot about calling your local crisis intervention hotline when problems seem too big to handle alone.

"That's for me," Brenda said. "When I just can't stand it any more." Giggling, she read the number aloud as it flashed across the screen: "Two-three-six, H-E-L-P!"

"You'll see him tomorrow at lunch, even if he doesn't call tonight," I said.

She thumped me with a pillow. "I don't want to hear about it. He *has* to call tonight, or — " Right on cue, the phone rang. Nearly overturning the bowl of potato chips, Brenda leaped up and bounded for the hall. She let the phone ring three more times before she picked it up and said, in a detached, formal voice, "Hello?" —I held my breath through the brief pause, waiting. Then Brenda gave a bubbling little laugh of delight. She actually managed to sound surprised when she exclaimed, "David! Hi! What's happening?"

The commercials were over at last. Now two women stood in a hospital corridor, arguing fiercely over which of them had the right to go in and see John. I tried to follow the story, not to eavesdrop on Brenda out in the hall. She stretched the phone cord around the corner into the living room, retreating as far from the den as possible for privacy. I couldn't catch enough words to follow the thread of the conversation, but now and then a peal of laughter cut across the drama of the intensive care unit.

After a while I went to the window and peered out at the lawn, washed in twilight. Brenda showed no signs of hanging up any time soon. I was tired of waiting for her. She seemed to have forgotten that I was there, that I even existed.

Brenda didn't glance up until I tapped her shoulder. "I've got to go," I whispered.

She nodded absently. "Mm-hmm," she murmured into the phone. "Me, too. I love it."

" 'Bye," I said, but she didn't answer me. Again I had that strange, faraway feeling, as though we didn't really know each other at all.

Last year Brenda listened to my joys and woes all the way through my crush on Ian McKay. Now it was her turn. It was ridiculous for me to feel jealous and left out, just because she was so excited over David.

No matter how reasonably I talked inside my head, there was an ache deep in my chest that didn't go away. It wasn't only Brenda and David. Everything was going wrong this year. I couldn't keep track of all the new people at school, I was slipping further and further behind in my classes, and I was a disaster whenever we played volleyball in p.e. And running through it all, too terrible to speak out loud, was this sense of dread about my eyes.

Automatically I crossed Brenda's backyard and started up the path through the woods. Dry leaves crackled underfoot, and the late afternoon rays slanted down through the bare autumn branches. A convention of crows shouted their greeting overhead. There was no time today to saunter along, watching the birds and squirrels and looking for bright patches of wildflowers. In just a few minutes the sun would set, and I would be in the dark.

Even as I hurried toward home, the dark trees seemed to draw closer. The path narrowed before my eyes as the sun sank in the sky. I should have taken the long way around by the road — at least the headlights of passing cars would help show me the way. It was too late to double back now. I might still reach our yard before dark, if I hurried.

Hurry! Hurry! I tried to drive my feet forward, but they had a will of their own. Slowly and cautiously they felt their way along the path, seeking out the clear space between the borders of underbrush. If only I had a flashlight! If only I had left Brenda's house ten minutes sooner! If only I hadn't let myself get careless, forgetting for a few crucial moments that I couldn't take the shortcut at dusk anymore.

Somewhere up ahead, I knew that a big log lay across the path. I strained to glimpse its great gray bulk, but by now I could scarcely see the ground in front of me. I found the log the hard way, with my right knee. My hand ripped through a bramble bush as I tumbled forward and a twig raked across my cheek.

"Stupid!" I muttered out loud. There was no one but the crows to hear me. "You're really in a mess this time! What are you going to do now?"

For a minute or two I just sat on the ground, nursing my scratches and bruises. A wind whipped through the trees, and I felt suddenly chilled all over. Tears scalded my eyes. It was just too dark. I couldn't grope my way another step. I was all alone, and so cold!

When I didn't show up for supper, Mom would phone Brenda's house. Unless Brenda was still tying up the line talking to David, Mom would find out that I had left an hour ago, and she'd send Melissa to look for me. I'd hear the snap of branches, impatient footsteps tramping through the leaves, and then her voice hollering, "Tracy! Where are you? Come on, Mom's getting all upset! She's got the food on!"

I couldn't let Melissa find me here, huddled in a heap against the log. She'd know at a glance that something was seriously the matter, and she'd race the news straight back to Mom and Dad. Once again I'd be her hopeless little sister, always in a mess, always causing problems. Her embarrassing little sister who couldn't manage to do the simplest thing right, not even see.

Shakily I pushed myself to my feet. I explored the log with both hands. It stretched as far as I could reach on either side, immense and immovable and covered with rough, craggy bark. If I tried to walk around it I might lose the path completely. It made more sense to climb over it, the way I always did in the daylight.

Carefully, holding my breath, I swung my right leg up and over. For a second I straddled the log, then swung my left leg over, too, and stood on flat, clear earth that had to be the path again. To my dismay I found that I hated to let go of the log. It was something solid in this blank wilderness with its nameless pitfalls. But I'd never get home if I didn't keep moving. And I had to get home, or everyone would find out. . . . For a last moment my hand lingered on a smooth patch of bark. Then I drove myself forward on my tortured journey, my feet scraping through the leaves to seek out the way other humans had cleared before me.

Up ahead I heard the faint gurgle of the brook, and with a pang of horror I remembered the little plank bridge. I'd missed the log, even though I was looking for it. If I missed the bridge, I'd be knee-deep in that icy water, twisting my ankles on the rocks at the bottom.

Step by step, the splashing, bubbling sound drew nearer, until I could bear the mounting dread no longer. On impulse I crouched down and began to crawl like a baby, feeling the way with my hands. If anyone came along now and saw me, I would lie down and bury myself in the mud with shame — but it really was easier. My hands told me the texture of the path, its worn clear places, the spots where it was broken with rocks. I discovered a hole, which could have snared my foot, and a tangle of branches, which I pushed out of the way.

The brook was louder now, throwing back echoes as it tumbled between its steep banks. Then my right hand found not damp earth and stones, but the hardness of rough weathered wood. The bridge was only three feet wide. Gingerly I touched the edge on either side, trying not to picture the drop to the water below. Like a clown's rendition of a tightrope walker, I centered myself on the plank and crept out over the stream. Hands first, knees and toes — I was entirely on the bridge now, inching clumsily along until my hands found earth and pebbles once more, and I had reached safety at last.

It was wonderful to be back on solid ground. The worst of the journey was behind me. But as soon as I stood up and started to walk again, I missed the messages my hands had been able to give me. If only there were a way I could walk upright and still be able to get some clues about where I was going.

Something slapped my left side. My hand

flew out to defend me and discovered a long, slender stick protruding from the underbrush. Before I thought out what I was doing, I yanked it free and held it out in front of me like a giant antenna. I felt it smack the bushes on either side of the path, but it showed me emptiness straight ahead, a clear path where I could walk freely.

I walked more quickly now, lured by the promise of home and light. I experimented with the stick, sometimes waving it in the air from side to side, sometimes scraping it over the ground in search of rocks and gullies. The trail dipped lower, then climbed the hill toward the end of our property. I strained my eyes into the distance, struggling to read the darkness — and suddenly I saw a glimmer of light.

I scrambled up the last rise, pebbles rolling underfoot, and broke from the woods onto our wide, level back lawn. Dogs barked off to the right, and the light shone straight before me. Flinging my stick into the bushes, I followed its beam as if I were a lost ship coming to harbor at last.

"Tracy," Mom called from the back door. "Come in and set the table. Your father's home and we're almost ready to eat."

I wondered how I would explain the muddy knees of my slacks and the scratches on my hands and face, but she didn't seem to notice. "He's got a meeting at eight, and I have to go talk to a Kennel Club group, and I just burned the rolls!" she lamented, opening the oven. "Can you clean up after supper? I just won't have time."

"Sure, Mom," I said. I would have been happy to agree to anything. I was home!

I couldn't go on like this any longer, tripping over logs, crawling on my hands and knees. I'd have to tell Mom that something was still wrong with my eyes, no matter how ugly my next glasses might be.

"Mom," I said, my voice coming out thin and feeble. "Mom, I — "

"Now what?" she demanded, half-turning with the pan of charred rolls in one hand.

I swallowed hard. "Nothing," I said. "Nothing important."

I studied my face in the bathroom mirror. A thin scratch ran down my right cheek from my ear to my jaw, but when I washed away the flecks of dried blood and brushed my hair forward a little it was almost hidden. My knuckles were pretty skinned up, but I was always getting bumps and cuts roughhousing with the dogs. There was no way anyone would know what had happened to me this afternoon unless I told the story myself.

I'd never take the shortcut through the woods at night again. From now on, I'd avoid any situation where I had to move around in the dark. I wouldn't have to tell Mom or Dad or Melissa, or Brenda or any of the kids at school. If I was always careful, all of the time, no one would find out what was happening to me. No one would have to know.

Chapter 6

In grammar school the teacher always handed out report cards on a Wednesday afternoon, and we carried them home in dread or relief for our parents to sign. At Millbrook High they didn't trust us to bear the news ourselves. Four times a year report cards arrived on Friday mornings, by mail. Mine awaited me in all its glory on the dining room table when I reached home after school.

Gingerly I picked it up between my fingertips, as though it might burn me. The envelope had been torn open already, so I knew Mom had looked it over. Fearfully I glanced down the column of grades: C, C, B+, C, D. . . .

D! My hands shook as I read it again: Algebra — D. I'd gotten very few C's in my career, and I had never received a D in my entire life.

There were none of the personal comments that the teachers used to write back in grammar school. Each grade was simply followed by a coded number that the computer could understand. My algebra teacher had awarded me a 6: "Inattentive." I had 6's in social studies and Spanish, too. After my C in English Mrs. Blanchard gave me a 3: "Homework."

My best grade was an A-minus in, of all things, physical education. I was a calamity on the volleyball court, I didn't make it in basketball or field hockey, and I found things to trip over whenever I walked across the gym. But Ms. Corona must have recognized effort when she saw it. In her generosity she had given me the best grade on my whole report card. *Ludicrous*, that's what it was. (I was *still* keeping up with my vocabulary homework, at least). It was just plain ludicrous. I gazed at that shining A-minus and began to giggle.

"I don't see anything very funny," Mom said from the doorway. "Your report card is a disgrace!"

"I'm sorry — I mean, I know," I stammered. "I just — I can't — "

"You know you can do better than this!" Mom snatched the report card and studied it again, shaking her head. "What do you do in class all day, look out the window?"

"No," I protested. "I pay attention, really. It's just — I don't know — everything goes so fast. I feel like I'm in a race and I can't keep up."

Mom looked at me accusingly. "Are you wearing your glasses at school? If you can't see the board — "

"I wear them all the time!" I was used to them now. In fact, sometimes I felt safe behind them, as if they were a shield to protect me from the world. As long as I was wearing glasses people didn't ask any dangerous questions about what I could or couldn't see.

Mom was no exception. "Well," she said, "if it isn't your vision, then what *is* the problem?"

All day I had tried to think of some excuse, anything to head Mom and Dad away from the truth. "I guess I just have to work harder," I said meekly. "It's rough getting used to high school. Everything's so different."

"We better see some real improvement next marking period," she said darkly. But her voice softened a little as she added, "Maybe you just need time to make the adjustment. High school's a lot more demanding than what you're used to."

"I'll say," I exclaimed. "I'll get my grades up somehow, don't worry."

"You will, or else," Mom said. She put down

my report card, her mind shifting to other things. "I've got to run over to the vet by four-fifteen," she said. "Annie's not eating, and her coat looks kind of blah. I'd better get going, the traffic'll be getting heavy."

When Mom was gone, I sank into a chair and rested my chin on my hand. How was I going to keep my promise and bring my grades up? If I got all C's and D's again next time, Mom and Dad wouldn't take any excuses. Almost anyone (except a paragon like Melissa) could daydream in class or get lazy about homework assignments; that was within the range of the normal. But I could just imagine how upset Mom and Dad would be if they guessed what was really wrong with me. And if they found out, the kids at school would know, too. How could I fit in, once they knew I was half-blind? They'd start avoiding me the way they avoided Sheila McGraw.

Upstairs Melissa practiced one phrase over and over again, honing it to perfection — a long, mournful sigh of strings, broken at the end, only to begin once more like some sorrow that could never be healed. Its sadness echoed deep within me, and a lump rose in my throat. What was really happening to me? I couldn't endure it alone for one more minute! But I couldn't talk about my eyes with anyone. Mom and Dad and Melissa lived in a different world, where they kept everything tightly under control. Brenda was floating on a cloud with David. And Craig — he was great when it came to Sasha's obedience training, but how could you share something so personal with a mad scientist?

Suddenly I pictured the den at Brenda's house, the couch where I had curled up with a Coke in my hand. "That's for me," Brenda had said. "When I just can't stand it any more." And a telephone number flashed through my mind. . . .

What would happen if I called the crisis hotline? They wouldn't be able to help me anyway, nobody could do that. Still, if I could only talk to someone, *anyone*, maybe I wouldn't feel so desperately alone.

Mom's station wagon rumbled out of the driveway. Dad wouldn't be home before six. Upstairs Melissa's violin sighed and lamented. No one would overhear me if I spoke to a stranger on the phone and said those terrible words.

I tiptoed into the kitchen and lifted the receiver from its hook. My heart pounded as the dial tone blared in my ear. Then, not giving myself time to think, I punched the numbers: two-three-six, H-E-L-P.

I counted the faraway rings — one . . . two . . . I'd hang up if they didn't answer by four. . . .

"Crisis hotline, Lynne speaking. Can I help you?"

It was a woman's voice, warm but business-like. My mind went blank. I couldn't find a word to say.

"Hello? Can we help you?" the voice repeated.

This was a ridiculous mistake. I'd hang up and forget I'd ever tried anything so dumb.

"You've reached the crisis intervention hotline," Lynne tried once more. "Would you like to talk to someone about a problem?"

"Is this real?" My voice came out louder than I expected, and suddenly I was ready to burst into giggles at one more ludicrous situation.

"Well, it really is a crisis hotline. Is that what you mean?" Lynne sounded youngish, and now I caught a little tinge of amusement under her words.

"What I meant was, what is this exactly? On TV they said to call up if you've got a problem you can't handle alone."

"Well, what we are, exactly, is a group of counselors who are here to talk to anyone who calls in," the voice explained. "Have you got something on your mind that you want to talk over with someone?"

"I think I shouldn't have called," I said. "My problems aren't anything much, really. I don't want to waste your time."

"You wouldn't be wasting my time. I'm here to listen."

There was a long pause. Somewhere across the wires someone waited to hear the words that burned in my thoughts day and night, but I couldn't speak them aloud. Still, I had to say something. "Well," I began, "I got a lousy report card today. All C's and D's. It's the worst one I ever got in my life."

"I can see you might be upset about that," Lynne said. "What's been going on?"

"I'm not doing anything right this year," I said. "I just started high school and I really hate it. My mother says maybe I need time to adjust, but I don't think I ever will."

"What makes it so hard?" Lynne asked. "What are the main things you have to adjust to?"

"There's too much work, that's all." I hesitated, then added in a rush, "And there are too many kids. I can't even learn all their names. And the whole place is so big I still get lost. Sometimes I get so mixed up I can't remember where I'm going."

"High school can be pretty overwhelming," Lynne agreed. "You feel like you're the only one who still gets mixed up — but I think just about everybody has that problem during the first few months."

"My friends sure don't act lost," I said. "And Melissa didn't have any problems her freshman year. She's my sister — she's a senior now."

"How can you be so sure?" Lynne said. "You would have been in about sixth grade when Melissa started high school, right? How can you remember what it was like for her?"

"I don't have to remember. I just know."

Abruptly the violin fell silent. Had Melissa heard me talking about her through the music? Footsteps creaked overhead, and I poised, ready to slam down the receiver if Melissa's feet reached the stairs.

"She must be quite a girl." Lynne's voice was almost teasing. "How can you just know that much about her?"

In the room above me the footsteps ceased. The silence stretched taut — and then the violin began again. Still, just to be safe, I lowered my voice and spoke close to the mouthpiece. "She does everything right all the time. She's beautiful, and she's got this neat boyfriend named Michael. And — hear that music?"

I held the receiver up toward the ceiling to

catch the strains of Bach. "Could you hear it?" I repeated. "That's her."

"She likes classical music? Listens to — "

"Not just listens. She *plays* it. Right now she's getting ready for her audition at the Juilliard School in New York. That's the best music school in the whole world, and she's going to go there."

I stopped to let Lynne tell me how proud I must be. Instead she asked, "What's it like, living with a sister like that?"

"It's — it's — well, sometimes it's really a pain." I stopped short. It was one thing complaining to Brenda about life with Melissa and her vast circle of admirers. But I felt like a traitor, talking that way to a complete outsider.

"You feel like you're always in her shadow?" Lynne filled in for me.

"Yeah," I muttered. "Something like that."

"It's hard when your sister or brother has some really outstanding ability that everyone makes a fuss over," Lynne said. "What you need to think about, though, are your own talents. The things you especially like, the things you're good at."

"I'm not much good at anything," I said. "Just look at my report card."

"You got good grades last year, didn't you?"

"Uh-huh. But not this year."

"Well, maybe you could use a little extra help for a while. What subject gives you the most trouble?"

"Algebra," I said. "I just don't get it." I almost added that I couldn't read the equations the teacher was always scribbling on the blackboard, but I caught myself in time.

"You could find out whether your school's got a tutoring program," Lynne suggested. "If someone helped you an hour or two a week, it might make a difference."

"I don't think so," I said. "Being smarter than I am, that's what would help."

Lynne seemed determined to find something hopeful about me. Nothing I said could stop her. "Okay, school's a bummer right now," she conceded. "What do you really like?"

"I like dogs." It was the first thing that popped into my head. I knew it sounded silly, like something a four-year-old might come up with. I hurried to explain. "My mother runs a kennel, raising show dogs. I like to help take care of them. And I'm trying to train my own dog. You know, for obedience trials."

"Oh yeah?" Lynne's voice sparkled with interest. "That sounds fascinating. Have you entered any yet?"

"No, we're just getting started. I might enter her in novice class competition in March. She ought to be ready by then."

"It must take a lot of patience," Lynne said. "You have to set aside time every day?"

"I give her Sundays off," I told her. "I do get a little down sometimes, when she has a bad day and doesn't remember anything. But mostly I keep at it, and she's doing okay."

"It sounds like you have a real knack for that sort of thing," Lynne said.

Right away I saw where she was heading the conversation. "It's not a special talent, like playing the violin," I said. "I just do it because it's fun."

"Sounds like an okay reason to me," Lynne said.

Again the violin stopped playing. This time I heard Melissa's door open, and she stepped out onto the landing at the top of the stairs. In another minute she would walk into the kitchen for one of her celery stalks. "I'm going to have to go," I said hastily. "I can't talk any more."

"Think about the things we discussed," Lynne said. "And give us a call again sometime. Let us know how school is going, how you and Melissa are getting along — "

Melissa's footsteps started down the stairs. "Okay, I will. But I've got to hang up now."

"Someone's coming? Is that why you can't talk?"

Melissa had reached the foot of the stairs. She crossed the dining room and stood in the kitchen doorway. "Mm-hmm," I said into the phone. "You've got it. 'Bye."

"Good-bye," Lynne said. "Hope to hear from you again."

"Who was that — Brenda?" Melissa asked as I set down the phone.

"No," I said. "Somebody else."

Melissa didn't pursue it any further. She headed straight for the refrigerator and pulled out the vegetable drawer.

Sasha trotted out from her favorite spot under the kitchen table. Her nylon bone stuck comically out of both sides of her mouth. "Come on, pup," I said. "Let's go do your workout."

I took a ball of twine from the cupboard and fastened one end to the ring of her choke collar. "Sasha, heel," I commanded, and she walked gracefully by my side into the living room.

In our obedience class we had progressed to the exercise called the long sit. Of course it was more challenging in class, with the distractions of eight or ten other dogs fidgeting around us. Even so, I could practice the "stay" and "come" aspects at home.

"Sit," I said, and Sasha sat back on her haunches, looking up at me with one ear on the alert. Unwinding the twine as I went, I backed the length of the room and called, "Sasha, come."

I didn't even have to tug the cord to remind her. Sasha stepped daintily forward until she stood directly in front of me. The bouncy puppy that rolled on the ground biting her leash was gone. She gazed up at me, intelligence and dignity shining in her face. She was perfect.

"Good girl!" I exclaimed, patting her head. Perhaps Lynne was right. Maybe training dogs did take a special talent, a talent I'd never thought about before.

I hadn't told Lynne about the most important problem I had, the one that haunted me day and night. But even talking about the little things helped a bit. Whoever she was, Lynne had a knack for saying things that made me feel better. And I hadn't even remembered to thank her.

Chapter 7

"Okay, Tracy," Ms. Corona said briskly. "Once more. Up and over you go!"

Gripping the high bar, I pushed off with my feet and rolled through a forward somersault. For one long, smooth moment I was in flight, coasting on air. Then my feet found the low bar and I came to rest, a creature of earth again.

"That was excellent," Ms. Corona said, helping me dismount. "You're a natural."

"Me?" I exclaimed, giggling. "You mean a natural disaster."

I couldn't sound too pleased, not with Brenda and Nancy right behind me. They'd think I was weird, getting enthusiastic about p.e. class. But Ms. Corona's compliment sent a little tingle of delight all through me. On the days when we did gymnastics, I actually enjoyed p.e. Swinging from the parallel bars or vaulting over the horse, I didn't have to worry about missing a ball or colliding with someone I didn't see.

I was happy and relaxed as I stood before the mirror in the locker room, combing the snarls out of my hair. It was turning out to be a good day. For one thing, I'd taken Lynne's advice and asked for a tutor in algebra. The guidance office assigned me to a senior honors student named Lori. I spent a week dreading our first session, sure she would make me feel more stupid than I did already. But when we finally met that morning during my study hall, Lori treated math like a fascinating puzzle. By the end of the period I found myself fitting a few of the pieces into place.

"He did? Really? You mean it?" Sheila McGraw's voice exploded behind me, shrill with excitement. "What did he say? Tell me just exactly!"

Usually Sheila sat by herself, or hovered longingly at the edge of a crowd. Now, to my amazement, she stood at the center of a laughing cluster of girls, all talking at once. "He said he thinks you're cute. Those are his exact words," Nancy was saying as I edged closer. "He said it's too bad the girls are supposed to ask the boys to that dance next month. He said if he could, he'd invite you to go with him."

I slipped in beside Brenda and gave her a nudge. "Who?" I whispered. "What's going on?"

"Tim Thatcher," she explained in a low voice. "Sheila's got a crush on him. He was talking to Nancy this morning about her."

In the murky lighting it was hard to read Brenda's face, but something in her tone was wrong.

"He said that to you, Nancy?" Sheila cried. "Honest? You're not putting me on?"

"I told you," Nancy said, giggling. "Those are his exact words. I wouldn't make it up."

"You think I should — you know — invite *him*?" Sheila asked. Even I could see the deep scarlet that flooded her face.

"Sure! Call him up!" Nancy urged.

"Go ahead! Call him!" added one of the other girls, whose face was half-hidden in shadow.

"I don't know," Sheila said. "I'd be too embarrassed."

"Why?" Nancy demanded. "You like him, don't you?"

"Well, yeah," Sheila mumbled. "But — "

"Well then you shouldn't waste a chance like this," Brenda put in.

"Maybe," Sheila said. "Maybe I can." Somehow the hope in her voice made me ache inside.

"What in the world was that about?" I demanded when Brenda and I reached the corridor.

"It was Nancy's idea," she said a little defensively. "She was talking to Tim this morning in assembly, and Sheila was across the room gazing at him, all adoration like she does. And Tim made all these sarcastic cracks about her being the cutest girl in the whole school and wanting to go to the dance with her and — "

"Oh, no!" I stared at her, horrified. "Why? Why did you let Nancy — ?"

"Nancy was telling the truth," Brenda insisted. "Word for word, that's just what he said!"

"But it isn't what he meant! What if she really calls him up tonight? He'll shoot her down!"

"It's just a joke," Brenda said impatiently. "Where's your sense of humor lately?"

"Sense of humor?" I repeated, confused. I couldn't believe they had done that to Sheila. I didn't see what my sense of humor had to do with it.

"You never want to have fun anymore," Brenda stated. "Like walking out in the middle of my party. And you never want to hang out at my house after school — "

"I do, too," I exclaimed. "I was there the day before yesterday!"

"Yeah, big deal. I think you stayed half an hour."

I always thought up an excuse now to hurry away before dark. I had to feed the dogs because Mom was out, or we were driving down to Morristown to have dinner with my aunt — but my stories weren't good enough. Brenda didn't buy them anymore.

We reached the branch in the hall where I had to turn to go down to Mrs. Blanchard's room. On a rising tide of panic, I wanted to whirl and run, to put a swarm of people and miles of corridor between me and Brenda's angry words. But if I fled, I would make her angrier than ever. I had to answer her, I had to say something.

What would happen if I told her the truth? Brenda, I'd say, I have to get home before sundown because as soon as it's dark I can't see my own two feet. . . .

It would never work. Brenda thought Nancy's trick on Sheila was a good joke, because Sheila was awkward and always said the wrong things. Brenda liked people who were just like her, who wore the same clothes and loved the same music and laughed at the same things she thought were funny. It was dangerous to be different.

"You never want to do anything after

school," she was saying. "And the other day I waved to you in the hall and you didn't even wave back."

"You did? I don't remember — I didn't see you."

"Yeah, sure," Brenda said. "I was right across the hall from you, you *had* to see me. Anyway, everybody says you're getting strange."

A cold finger of dread slithered down my spine. My knees began to shake. "What do you mean? Who says?"

"Nancy and Joanne and everybody. You walk around with your nose in the air half the time, like you think you're better than the rest of us."

"Brenda, I do not!" I wouldn't let her make me cry, I wouldn't — but my eyes burned with tears.

Right over our heads the bell rang, a long, piercing clamor. Brenda and I faced each other in the nearly empty hall. "It's not just me," she declared. "Everybody says so, so you know it's true."

I was cornered. I couldn't escape into another story. But I knew more clearly than ever that I couldn't tell anyone what was really wrong.

* * *

I ran down to my locker after school, but Brenda wasn't waiting to meet me. I told myself she was probably going somewhere with David instead, but it didn't ease the hurt in my chest. In a daze I walked home alone.

I hardly heard the joyful greeting of the dogs in their runs as I trudged up the driveway. I was on the porch, rummaging for my key, when Craig called, "Tracy! Over here!"

I brushed my hand across my face as though to clear away cobwebs, and stared toward the voice. Craig emerged from the puppy run, a squirming ball of fur in his arms.

"Craig!" I said, struggling to pull my thoughts together. "I forgot you were coming over today."

"Good thing I didn't," he said. "Where's Sasha, in the house?"

"Yeah. I've been keeping her in most of the time, trying to civilize her."

"Is it working?"

"Sometimes. Sometimes not. Yesterday she chewed the leg of a chair half off." I heard my voice across a vast distance, as if I were talking in my sleep.

Sasha was waiting when I pushed the door open. She hurled herself upon me, wriggling all over with joy. For a few moments my misery over Brenda faded into the background. I crouched on the carpet and gave Sasha a big hug, barely fending off her frantic attempts to lick my face. At least Sasha didn't wonder why I was acting strange, or imagine that I looked down on everyone around me. At least Sasha thought I was fun.

At last I stood up and went automatically to the dining room table where Mom always left the mail. Behind me I heard Craig roughhousing with Sasha while I flipped halfheartedly through the bills and magazines. I was about to toss aside an envelope from the Kittatinny Kennel Club, certain it was for Mom, when I saw that it was addressed to me.

"Here's a brochure about novice matches," I said, tearing open the envelope. "And Sasha's application! Her application for her first obedience trial."

"What does it say?" Craig asked eagerly. "Does she qualify and all that stuff?"

I stepped over to the window and read swiftly in the soft afternoon light. "Let's see — any purebred dog over six months of age . . . Kennel Club officials and members of their families not eligible to . . . handler must be thoroughly familiar with Novice Class regulations . . . Yeah, it looks like she can enter, according to this. I'd better send this in right away. Mom says sometimes they fill up really fast and quit taking applications."

The form wasn't complicated. Sasha's full kennel name looked truly impressive when I wrote it out: Hickory Road's Empress Sasha. Mom had laughed when I made up the "Empress" part, but I liked giving Sasha a touch of royalty in spite of her droopy ear.

"Done," I said, signing my name at the bottom of the sheet. "I'll mail it tomorrow on the way to school."

Craig picked up the letter that had come with the application. "April 4th at 8 PM," he mused. "That gives you almost four months — "

"Eight o'clock?" I cried. "They never hold trials at night! I never heard of such a thing!" I snatched the letter from Craig and read it myself, *8 PM.* How had I overlooked it before? It would be dark outside. Even inside the auditoriums the lighting would probably be too dim. I'd bang into chairs and step on dogs and trip over leashes. . . .

Craig was so busy studying the brochure that he didn't notice my dismay. "This is great. It's got all the exercises laid out, and the orders the judges give and everything. Hey, I'll be the judge. I'll tell you just what you've got to do."

Numbly I followed him into the living room. Craig said it didn't look much like the ring in the photo, even after we pushed back the coffee table and a couple of chairs to make more space, but it would have to do. "Okay," he said. "First let's do the heel on leash and the figure eight. Are you ready?"

"I guess so." I snapped the leash to Sasha's collar. "Come on, girl. Let's go. Heel."

"Wait a second. You're not allowed to talk that much. You just give her one command, remember?"

I drew Sasha around to my left side, and she waited expectantly. "Sasha, heel," I told her. Sasha trotted forward, sticking close to my left side just as I had taught her.

"Halt," Craig commanded in the voice of a general.

I stopped short, but Sasha marched ahead to the length of her leash before she slowly sat down.

"I'm afraid I've got to take off two points for that one," Craig said. "Sasha, you can do much better than that!"

Sasha laid her ears back and looked sorrowfully from Craig to me. "Don't worry," Craig said. "I don't know why it's got to be so precise. It says here when the judge says 'Halt,' you should both stop instantly, and Sasha's got to sit without any command from you. She should sit just because you stopped walking."

We worked for almost an hour, on heel on leash, heel free (without a leash), Figure 8 around two straight chairs, and the long sit. Whenever I praised her, Sasha's ear pricked up and she wagged her tail with delight. As she got into the spirit of the game, I praised her more and more often. But all the time I knew it was no use.

"Don't forget to mail in that application right away," Craig reminded me as he went to get his coat. "You wouldn't want to miss the deadline."

I stared at the flowered pattern in the carpet. I had to tell him today, before he got any more enthusiastic. But he'd never understand. "Craig," I said in a thin, tight voice, "I'm not going to enter her after all."

"What?"

Slowly I lifted my eyes to meet his gaze. He was staring at me, the picture of disbelief. "What do you mean you're not going to enter her!" he cried. "What did you fill out that form for? Why did you work with her this afternoon?"

"I just don't want to." I groped desperately for some explanation that would make sense. "She's still just fourteen months old. Most of the shepherds don't start going to matches till they're two — "

"So what? She's doing great."

"I know, but — " There was no story I could offer. But I couldn't tell him the truth. "I can't explain it. It just — just doesn't feel right. Like it's not the right time to do it or something."

Craig shook his head doubtfully. "You think you'll enter her later? In some other show?"

"Sure," I said with relief. "Maybe later. Like in the summer." In the summer they might use an outdoor ring, lit with clear golden sunshine.

"Well, okay, I guess." Craig wasn't quite appeased. "We can still work on her training then, can't we?"

I nodded. "I don't want to quit working with her," I tried to explain. "It's just — I think it's too soon. Like you said, everything's got to be so precise, I don't want to pressure her too much."

Craig didn't argue any more, but I knew he was baffled. "Okay if I take all this stuff that came in the mail?" he asked, pausing on his way to the door. "I can go over those judges' rules."

"Why not?" I handed him the envelope, with all of the material stuffed back inside, and waved good-bye as he disappeared across the yard into the darkness.

I sank onto the couch and curled into a ball, my chin in my hands. Sasha wasn't allowed on the furniture, but I didn't bother to scold her when she leaped up beside me. I needed her company.

After a while the doorbell rang, and Melissa swept downstairs to greet Michael. She shouted something to me over her shoulder about running out to the mall, and they were gone. Sasha and I were alone in the big, echoing house.

"What am I going to do, Sasha?" I asked, rubbing her behind the ears. "Things are worse all the time."

Sasha licked my hand, but that didn't answer my question. Only people could give answers, but I couldn't tell my problems to anybody I knew.

Slowly I uncurled and got to my feet. Sasha followed me out to the kitchen, hoping it was time for her supper. She flopped down with a resigned sigh when I picked up the phone and dialed two-three-six, H-E-L-P.

"Crisis hotline, Lynne speaking," said a familiar, businesslike voice in my ear.

"Hi! I didn't think it'd be you again!" I said

in surprise. "I mean, I thought, since there must be lots of people that answer the phones over there — "

"I wouldn't say there are lots of us. Just a few, really," Lynne said. "Refresh my memory. Who are you?"

My heart sank. I remembered everything she'd said to me, and she had forgotten that I existed. "Tracy," I said dully. "I talked to you a couple of weeks ago. I'm the one with the sister who's a violinist — "

"Oh, sure! I know who you are now. How are you?"

She sounded so happy to hear from me that I felt better right away. "I'm fine," I said. "I mean, in some ways I'm fine, at least. I'm getting tutored in math and I think it'll help."

"Good," said Lynne. "What else is going on in your life?"

Now was my chance to tell her. Maybe once I spoke the words, they wouldn't be quite so terrifying. Oh, I'd say breezily, nothing much new, except I think I'm going blind. . . .

"I had a fight with my best friend this afternoon," I said. "It was really awful. We were friends since sixth grade and now I don't think she even wants to hang out with me anymore."

"How come?" Lynne wanted to know. "What's wrong?"

I twisted the telephone cord between my fingers. "She says I'm getting stuck-up, and I'm no fun to be around. She never used to say stuff like that."

"Your feelings must really be hurt," Lynne said. "Especially if you were always good friends."

"The thing is," I said, "sometimes I'm not sure I still even want her for a friend. She's starting to change."

"Change how?" Lynne asked.

I hadn't fully realized it before, but now that I put it into words, I knew I was right. "Since we started high school, she's — a little bit mean sometimes. She's always making fun of people who don't wear the right clothes, dumb stuff like that. And there's this one girl, she's not very popular — and Brenda picks on her this year." I paused, trying to think it out. "I don't trust her anymore, you know what I mean?"

"You see what she does to other people, and you think she could do the same to you," Lynne suggested.

"Something like that," I said. "Only — she was my best friend, and I haven't got anybody else. And it's pretty lonely."

"It's hard losing a friend," Lynne said. "But you know, there are a lot of other people out there for you to get to know this year. Do you belong to any clubs after school, sports, anything like that?"

"No. I'm about as athletic as a doughnut," I said, and we both laughed a little.

"Well, how about through your dog training?" Lynne asked. "Do you meet any other kids through that?"

"Not really," I said. "Craig helps me some, he's the boy down the road. But I already know him."

"Well, give it some thought," Lynne said. "Once you start making some new friends, you won't feel so bad about Brenda."

"Okay," I said uncertainly. "I'll think about it. I guess I'd better go."

"All right," Lynne said. "Call us any time."

"Good-bye," I said. And this time I remembered to say thank you.

Chapter 8

"We have a lot of ground to cover today," Mrs. Blanchard said in her squeaky old voice. "Let's start by running quickly through the vocabulary list. Just raise your hands and define the words as I call them out — beginning with *elusive*."

With a secret sigh of relief I settled back in my seat. At least I wouldn't have to make a trip to the blackboard today. I waited through the first three or four vocabulary words, not wanting to seem too eager, and finally waved my hand in the air when Mrs. Blanchard asked for the definition of *appalling*.

"All right, Tracy," she said. She always seemed to give my name a special emphasis. I had the uneasy feeling that she was keeping her eye on me.

"It means really awful," I said. "Dreadful. Terrible."

"Can you use it in a sentence?" Mrs. Blanchard asked.

I wanted to say, The lighting in this room is absolutely appalling! But I caught myself just in time. "Last night I sat through an appalling movie."

"Fine," Mrs. Blanchard said, and moved on to the next volunteer. With any luck, she would leave me in peace now for the rest of the period.

Appalling was precisely the word to describe the lighting in Room 231. The windows were on the east side of the building — the dark side by eighth period, when my class met. The overhead lighting was so dim I had to strain to make out large letters scrawled on the board. To read from a book on my desk I had to bury my face in the pages.

"Now time to move on to other things," Mrs. Blanchard chirped. She paused, thumbing through a stack of papers on her desk. My body went tense. What would it be next — flipping through the pages of the grammar book to find a hidden set of exercises? Deciphering instructions from a blurry Xeroxed work sheet? My mind raced ahead, searching for ways to survive every gruesome possibility.

"Take out your lit books," Mrs. Blanchard

said brightly. "Turn to the story 'The Man Who Could Work Miracles, by H G. Wells. That's on page 73."

I dragged the book from the rack beneath my seat and bent forward to see the page numbers. I was still hunting for page 73 when Mrs. Blanchard resumed, "One of the best ways to appreciate a story like this is to read it aloud. Why don't we all take turns, starting with Sue-Ann in the first row."

Through a fog of panic I heard one of the boys mutter, "What does she think this is, *Sesame Street*?" Soft and silent, a net of despair settled over me. In this light I could only read slowly, cautiously, checking to make sure each word was right. If I had to read out loud, I'd stumble like a first-grader. I could already feel the sharp, mocking glances, and hear the rising titters of laughter.

The words swam before me as I tried to follow Sue-Ann in my book. At last, when she reached the end of the first paragraph, Mrs. Blanchard said, "Continue down row one. Ralph, you're next."

Paragraph by paragraph, the story unfolded down the first row. It was something about a man who discovered he could make things happen just by willpower — but my mind was swirling in so many directions that I couldn't follow the plot. Maybe the bell would ring before my turn came. But no, there would be plenty of time. Wretchedly I counted heads — after Ralph there were nine people to go before Mrs. Blanchard would call on me. Everyone would know that even with my glasses I still couldn't see. . . .

Suddenly an idea leaped out at me, and I felt a surge of hope. Running my finger down the page, I counted and recounted the paragraphs to make certain. If Mrs. Blanchard didn't shift the pattern, the twelfth one would fall on me. Leaning over my desk as though I were drowsy with boredom, I read through it once slowly, fighting to stay calm. It was easier when I plunged into it the second time, and the words had a pleasing way of hanging together. I closed my eyes and recited the opening sentence inside my head: "He pointed resolutely to his candle and collected his mind, though he felt he did a foolish thing. . . ."

The paragraph was mercifully short, only five sentences. My feverish mind captured it line by line, until it was locked safely into my memory. Now only three people were left to read before my turn came. There would be Tim Thatcher, Marie Markowitz, and Sheila McGraw.

I covered the page with my hand and played

the entire paragraph in my mind. I heard real expression in the words now. I would roll them off my tongue like an actress, bringing the whole scene to life. No one would ever guess that I only pretended to read.

Marie read dully, as if the words were just empty sounds. She was nearly finished when the telephone by the door let out a long, demanding buzz. Mrs. Blanchard crossed the room and answered with a cheery, "Hello?"

The instant the teacher's back was turned, a flock of little whispers and giggles fluttered around the room. But the break lasted only a moment, before she hung up the receiver and turned back to us again. "Sheila," she said, "you're to report to the office."

I didn't notice if Sheila turned pale and trembling, the way I did whenever I got that sort of summons. Through a roaring like waves in my ears I heard her faint question, "Now?" and Mrs. Blanchard's faraway reply, "Right now."

The room swayed around me. My face flushed hot, but my hands were suddenly cold as ice. I knew what was coming, even before Mrs. Blanchard called to me across the pounding surf, "Tracy, will you read next, please?"

There was only one shred of hope left. I'd skip Sheila's paragraph eleven, and race into paragraph twelve so fast that Mrs. Blanchard wouldn't even notice. I drew a shuddering breath and began, "He pointed resolutely to his candle and — "

Mrs. Blanchard held up her hand. "Back up a little. Start up above, with — "

The words melted into a black smear across the page. I couldn't find where to begin. I was trembling all over now, my face flaming, and I knew I would never find the place.

I stared around me in terror. Everyone was looking at me, wondering what was wrong. I had to say something, anything to push all those probing eyes away. I opened my mouth and heard myself begin again: "He pointed resolutely to his candle, and collected his mind. . . ."

"Tracy?" Mrs. Blanchard's voice curled into a question. But I couldn't answer. The net tightened around me, and I had to break away before it dragged me down.

"I'm sorry — I can't — I have to go — " I scrambled to my feet, half-running for the door.

"Tracy!" Mrs. Blanchard shouted, but I didn't stop. I heard the rising murmur of voices at my back, a tide of astonishment that swept the whole room. Then I burst out into the long, empty corridor and slammed the door behind me.

I don't remember rushing down to my locker, but somehow I found myself there, pulling open the long metal door. In a daze I realized that my hands were strangely empty — I had left my books and notebooks at my desk in Mrs. Blanchard's room. It didn't matter. It was against the rules to dash out of class, to leave school before the three-o'clock bell gave permission, but that didn't matter either today. The net wrapped still tighter, tangling my thoughts into knots. I had to get out, get away somewhere.

A gust of wind struck me as I flung open the door to the parking lot. But even as I stepped breathless into the cold sunlight, I knew the net still held me in its grip. There was no escape to safety, no escape anywhere for me. Something appalling was about to happen.

The call came at eight-thirty that night. I remember the time exactly, because Mom had just looked at her watch and remarked that Dad's meeting must have run extra late, when his key turned in the front door. Sasha skidded across the vestibule and gave him such an enthusiastic greeting that he nearly dropped his briefcase. At that moment the telephone rang.

"I'll get it, it's Michael," Melissa called, and flew out to the kitchen.

Sasha ran to me, wagging with joy the way she always did when the whole family was together at last. I half listened as Dad told Mom about the big contract he had just won, to design a new shopping mall out on Route 23. In the kitchen Melissa's voice lifted in polite surprise, and I knew that it wasn't Michael on the phone.

"Oh, sure . . . Of course I do! I'm fine . . . Well, I'm keeping pretty busy . . . Sure, I will — nice talking to you again."

I heard her set the receiver down on the counter. She reappeared in the doorway and turned to Mom. Even before she opened her mouth, I knew what she was going to say. "One of the teachers from school is on the phone, wants to talk to you. It's Mrs. Blanchard."

"I'm not joining the PTA," Mom said, laughing. "Honestly, they shouldn't bother people at home."

"You don't have to talk to her," I exclaimed. "I bet she wants you to sell raffle tickets. They're trying to — " But with a shrug of her shoulders, Mom headed out to the kitchen.

Dad vanished into his office, but Melissa perched on one of the dining room chairs, watching me. "What's going on?" she asked in a low voice.

"Sshh!" I tiptoed to the doorway, straining for Mom's words.

"Yes, this is Jean Newbury." Her voice had a hard, businesslike edge. No time for raffle tickets or the PTA or —

"Blanchard sounds like more of a fuddy-duddy than ever," Melissa said. "What does she want, anyway?"

I shook my head, willing her to be quiet. "No, not really," Mom was saying. The brittle edge was gone now, and there was a tremor of anxiety in her tone. "We've been concerned about her grades, naturally, but . . . She *did*? She . . . No, but we'll discuss it. We certainly will. . . ."

"What in the world — " Melissa tried again.

"Nothing! Nothing! Never mind!" I shouted over my shoulder on a wild dash for the stairs. My room was the last haven left. I would hide behind the locked door, and no one could make me answer any questions. . . .

"Tracy," Mom said behind me. "Come here. I want to talk to you."

I don't know how long we stood there, frozen like people in a picture — me looking down with one hand on the curving wooden banister, Mom pinning me with a commanding stare that would make the most stubborn dog come and sit and stay. At the sound of my name, my will had drained away, leaving me hopeless and hollow.

"Tracy, what's this Mrs. Blanchard's telling me?" Mom asked as I stumbled back downstairs. "She said she wanted to make sure you were all right. She thought maybe you were sick all of a sudden."

I stared down at the carpet, struggling to collect my mind, like the man in paragraph twelve.

"She says you jumped up and ran out of the classroom today, for no reason," Mom went on. "But you had to have a reason. What was the matter?"

The office door opened and Dad emerged. "What's the problem?" he asked, taking us in with a worried glance.

"I just got a call from Tracy's English teacher," Mom said. "She says Tracy's been acting funny lately." She sounded utterly mystified.

"Funny?" Dad repeated blankly.

Melissa still watched, leaning in the background by Mom's antique sideboard. An odd thought bounced through my head — how peculiar it was to be the center of everyone's attention, to see Melissa forgotten out on the fringes.

"Tracy," Mom said. "What is all this about?" All three of them waited for me to speak, to enlighten them.

They had me in the net now, hands and feet so enmeshed I couldn't try to get away. I couldn't dodge behind excuses any longer.

"She wanted me to read out loud," I said, my voice barely above a whisper. "In front of everybody. And I couldn't."

"What do you mean, you couldn't?" Dad demanded. "You can read. You've always been a good reader."

I twisted my hands together but they wouldn't stop shaking. "It was so dark in there. I could hardly see the page."

"Well if it was dark, why didn't somebody put on the light?" Mom asked logically.

"Nobody else thought it was dark. Only me."

"Wait a minute," said Dad. "Let's get this straight. You're having trouble reading? Are you wearing your glasses?"

"I wear them! I wear them all the time!" My voice rose out of my control to a wail of despair. "The glasses don't help at all! I just can't see! I don't recognize people, and I bump into things all day long, and when it's dark I can't see anything!" I had to say it now. I couldn't keep back the terrible words any longer. "I think I'm going blind!"

Chapter 9

"You watch. It'll turn out to be nothing," Mom tried to promise me. She reached over and gave my knee an awkward pat.

"If it was nothing, why did the doctor call us in special to talk about those tests?" I asked. "Why did they want you and Dad both to be here, to talk about nothing?"

She couldn't answer that. She turned for help to Dad, but he was buried in a magazine. He hadn't had much to say for the past two weeks, ever since that disastrous night when Mrs. Blanchard had called.

As befitted a "top man in the field," Dr. Silverman had the nicest waiting room I had sat in so far. Dr. Abramowitz, the optometrist who prescribed my glasses, had stiff vinyl-covered furniture that crackled when you shifted your weight. Dr. Capano, the eye doctor he referred us to when Mom called him about my problems, had dusty plastic ferns and an ugly oil painting of a seascape. But here in Dr. Silverman's waiting room we sat on comfortable upholstered sofas, and lush green spider plants tumbled from hanging pots. There was even an aquarium on the far wall, where orange-and-yellow angelfish glided around and around in lazy circles.

But all three doctors chose the same lifeless canned music, and their offices all had the same faint medicinal smell that filled me with dread. When I closed my eyes, I couldn't tell one waiting room from another.

I turned quickly as a door clicked open. "Tracy Newbury?" the receptionist bubbled. "The doctor will see you now."

"Does he want her alone?" Mom asked, half-rising beside me. "Or should we — does he — ?"

"I think he'd prefer to meet with all of you together," the receptionist said with the same determined good cheer. "Come this way, please."

I tried to stand up, but my legs refused to move. Maybe Mom and Dad could go in without me and hear what the doctor had to say. Maybe I could stay here in my corner of the sofa and they could all just leave me alone. . . .

Mom and Dad must each have been thinking the same thing. For a few seconds all three of us sat motionless, as though the receptionist hadn't spoken. Then Dad tossed his magazine aside and got abruptly to his feet. "Okay, let's go," he said in a low, taut voice. Mom touched my shoulder and somehow I forced myself to stand, to set one foot in front of the other, to follow the receptionist through the door and down the narrow hall to Dr. Silverman's office.

The room was large and bright. Even from where I sat I could make out the lettering on the spines of some of the thick, somber-looking books that lined his shelves: *Diseases of the Retina* and *Surgical Intervention in Traumatic Injury to the Eye*. I twisted around in my chair to study the framed diplomas on the wall, and the bronze statue of a runner balanced on top of the bookcase. Directly above the doctor's broad, glass-topped desk hung a giant full-color poster of the human eye. I wanted to look at anything besides Dr. Silverman himself, looming before me, full of terrible knowledge.

Pages rustled as the doctor opened a thick blue folder. At last he spoke.

"In order for you to understand what I'm about to tell you, I have to explain a little bit about the mechanics of vision," he began in a quiet, detached voice. He rose to stand before the poster of the eye. "Now," he said, pointing, "the eye is very much like a camera. Light rays enter here — this is the pupil. They pass through the lens to the retina. The retina is a paper-thin lining at the back of the eye, which serves more or less as the camera's film. . . ."

He rambled on, pointing and explaining like a teacher in front of a drowsy class. I twisted my hands on my lap and let the empty words rattle at my ears. What did all of this have to do with why I tripped over chairs, why I got lost on a familiar path at night?

"Of course, it's all much more complex than that," Dr. Silverman went on. "I'm just giving you a very basic idea what goes on under normal circumstances. Is everything clear so far?"

"Yes, I believe so," said Dad. I could tell he was growing impatient. "What about all those tests and examinations? What about Tracy?"

I flinched at the sound of my name. I wished Dr. Silverman would talk about those parts of the camera forever, and forget about me.

"About Tracy," the doctor repeated thoughtfully. He settled back into his swivel chair. "Yes. I can give you her diagnosis. It's very straightforward, really." Yet still he thumbed through the folder on his desk, as though searching for the right words.

The room was unbearably hot. I wanted to ask Dr. Silverman to open the window, to let the February wind howl in on us. But I couldn't squeeze any sound out through my parched throat. I waited.

When Dr. Silverman finally spoke, his tone did not change. He was still trying to stuff information into a group of students who didn't seem to have read the assignment. "Tracy has a progressive condition that affects the retina — that's the eye's film, as I showed you in the diagram. The condition is called *retinitis pigmentosa*."

It has a name, I remember thinking in that first instant. This has all happened to other people before me. Then the doctor's words echoed through my mind and I tried to translate them into something I could understand. A "progressive condition that affects the retina. . . ." What did *progressive* mean? We'd never had it yet on one of Mrs. Blanchard's lists.

"What is the treatment?" Mom asked. "Will she have to take medication?"

There was a short, uneasy pause. "No," Dr. Silverman said at last. "I'm afraid that right now there is no treatment available."

No medication. No treatment. I couldn't attach any meaning to those simple words. Nothing the doctor said could affect me. None of it felt quite real.

But Dr. Silverman's words had a powerful effect on Mom. "You mean to tell us there's not a thing we can do?" she exclaimed. "We're living in the 1980s! There are all kinds of medical advances — "

"There's research going on all over the country," Dr. Silverman said. "We know that it's a genetic condition, a recessive trait carried by both parents — "

"A genetic condition!" Now Mom was truly outraged. "We've never had anything like this in the family before. On both sides, everyone has always had excellent eyesight. My grandmother never wore glasses until she was eighty-two! There has to be a mistake."

"Recessive traits can be passed on for generations before they appear," Dr. Silverman said. "The diagnosis is really very straightforward, as I said. There are distinctive changes in the retina characteristic of RP — we usually call it by its initials; *retinitis pigmentosa* is such a tongue-twister." Dr. Silverman gave a slight laugh, but no one else noticed the joke. "Right now your daughter has the two major symptoms of RP in its early stages. Her eyes don't adjust to the dark in the normal way — we call that night blindness. And she's lost quite a bit of peripheral vision, which means that she can't see off to the sides unless she turns her head. Looking straight in front of her, with good lighting, her vision is fine."

Mom fell silent, but I knew she was gathering her forces for the next assault. It was Dad who asked the next question, his voice almost as level as the doctor's. "What can we expect?"

"You have to understand that each case proceeds in its own unique way," Dr. Silverman replied. "There's no definite timetable, no set course."

"Look," Dad said, "we've got to hear whatever you can tell us. Will her vision stay the way it is now, or get worse, or — ?" The unspoken words quivered in the air between us all.

"She could stabilize at this plateau for years. I have one patient who's thirty-one, and she's still driving in daylight. Some of the patients I follow read regular print, using magnifying devices — "

"But she's unusual, that woman who can still drive?" My own voice took me by surprise, too loud, ringing with panic. "You mean, most people with what I've got — they can't even drive at all?"

For the first time Dr. Silverman spoke directly to me, as though there were no one else in the room. "You're going to have to deal with something pretty tough," he said. "But it isn't the end of the world, just remember that. You'll learn to live with it, live a normal life."

I nodded. Through the static in my head I heard him continue, "What RP does is slowly destroy the retinas of your eyes. You may have had it for two or three years, but the changes were so gradual you hardly noticed at first."

He wasn't really talking about me. He was describing someone else, a stranger with a progressive condition, whatever that was. But I nodded again, as if I followed every word, and waited for him to go on.

"You can reach a plateau, which means your vision may stay the same for months or even years. And then suddenly there can be a change, as more of the retina is damaged. With every change, your field of vision becomes narrower."

"Narrower?" I echoed. "You mean, I'll see less and less all the time? And then finally. . . ."

"Finally — eventually — it's quite likely that you will become blind."

Blind! The word hung in the air like a dagger, invisible yet deadly, pointed straight at the core of my being.

The heat in the room was unbearable now. I couldn't breathe. I had to get out. I turned to Mom, and like a little child I pleaded, "I want to go home."

"All right," Mom said, "I think we should go now." Gently she put her hand beneath my elbow, supporting me as I stumbled to my feet.

She turned to the doctor, and her voice was icy. "What about that optometrist who prescribed the glasses?" she demanded. "He said there was nothing seriously wrong with her eyes! Who are we supposed to believe?"

"At this stage you can't diagnose RP by having someone read an eye chart," Dr. Silverman explained. "It's a very common mistake — "

"Thank you for giving us your time," Dad said. "I think we should get another opinion."

Mom led the way as the three of us moved toward the door. "Yes, that's an excellent idea," Dr. Silverman was saying to our backs. "You need to know that you're doing everything you can. And there may be a breakthrough one of these days. There's some very promising research going on."

Mom opened the door and marched out into the hall. Dr. Silverman trailed after us, still talking. "You'll want to think about Braille at some point, and cane travel might be a good idea."

I forced my feet to go faster, to carry me away from his words. "Call any time," he went on. "Don't hesitate to come in any time you've got a question."

The smell of medicine was stronger in the hallway. It made my head reel. "I haven't got any questions," I said. "There's nothing else that I want to know."

Chapter 10

No matter how bad things got, Mom believed in family meals. On Sunday morning she insisted that I go downstairs for French toast, but the first mouthful tasted like cardboard and I pushed my plate away. After a few sips of orange juice I retreated back to my room again.

Dr. Silverman hadn't mentioned all the side effects of RP. It didn't only destroy the retinas. It kept you awake at night, made you cringe when people tried to talk to you, even stole your appetite for your favorite Sunday-morning breakfast.

I stretched out on my bed. Footsteps tiptoed lightly up and down the stairs, voices murmured into the telephone behind closed doors. Even Melissa's violin was silent — at a time like that music would have been out of place. The house had the hushed, heavy feeling that hung over it when we all came back after Grandma Newbury's funeral last summer. Nothing was missing but the flowers.

Always before I had had a hundred reasons to hurry. I rushed through chores around the house, trotted Sasha through her obedience exercises, dashed off to see Brenda or Craig, ran home for dinner, helped wash down the kennel, raced upstairs to do my homework. But ever since we came home from Dr. Silverman's office Friday afternoon, none of those things were important. My bed was an island where I lay marooned, remote from the ordinary things that still mattered to other people.

Most of the time I managed to keep my mind a blank, but every so often a new thought stung me. I wouldn't be able to put on my own lipstick if my eyes got worse. I wouldn't know what colors my clothes were. I might never be able to get my driver's license. Someone would always have to lead me by the hand like a little kid. Sometimes I surfaced from a misty half-dream with one vast, terrible word shouting through my brain: *blind!*

Now and then Mom peered around the door frame, trying to persuade me to eat something. Dad dropped in to tell me he was looking into things, he'd found out about an RP specialist in Boston who was up on all the latest developments. Melissa knocked once, but I never found out what she wanted. When I told her to go away, she shut the door and left me alone.

People always wanted to talk. They fired volleys of useless words, which they somehow believed would mend my spirit. Or even worse, they asked questions and waited for me to answer. "How are you feeling?" Mom would say, peering in at me. I couldn't explain that I was trying with all my strength to feel nothing, to think of nothing, to curl in upon myself and hide from the future.

Sasha was different. She flew at me in her usual exuberant greeting when I stumbled into the house after my appointment with Dr. Silverman. But almost immediately she must have sensed that something was wrong. Instead of scrambling onto my lap, she sat quietly beside me and leaned her head on my knee. She padded behind me wherever I went, and lay down at my feet if I sank into a chair. We both forgot the old rule which forbade her to get onto the bed. As I lay there in the twilight between waking and sleep, between knowing and oblivion, she stretched warm and soft beside me. I folded my arm over the lean smoothness of her back and hugged her close. Sasha offered me a consolation deeper than words.

"Tracy? Are you awake, hon?"

I sat up slowly, pushing my tangled hair back from my face, as Mom opened the door again. Was it lunchtime already? "I'm awake," I muttered.

"I didn't know," she said, stepping into the room. "That was just Brenda on the phone, and I told her you were sleeping."

I leaned over to glance at my watch on the night table. According to the digital readout, it was one thirty-nine PM. "You told her I was asleep?" I repeated. "What did she say?"

Mom picked up my hairbrush, turned it in her hands, and set it down. "She was kind of surprised," she admitted. "She wanted to know why you weren't up yet."

I could hear Brenda's voice inside my head, laughing with amazement, "She's not up *yet*? It's the afternoon!" And then, "What's the matter with her, anyway?"

Mom walked nervously to the window and straightened the curtains. I could barely move, but she couldn't seem to keep still. "What did you tell her?" I asked.

"I said you weren't feeling well." Mom hesitated, twisting the curtain cord into knots, and I knew something else was coming. "She was quite concerned," Mom went on. "She said you hadn't been feeling well lately — you never mentioned that to me! — and I explained that

127

you were having trouble with your eyes — "

"Mom! You didn't tell her that!"

"She's your best friend, isn't she?" Mom protested. "I thought if anybody — "

I was wide awake now, tingling and alert. "Sure, but you didn't have to mention my eyes."

Usually Mom was so definite, so unshakably sure of herself. But now she hesitated, backing away. Maybe she realized she'd made a disastrous mistake, and she wished she could go back and undo the harm — but it was too late. For an instant I felt sorry for her, she looked so trapped. But I had to know the truth, all of it. "What exactly did you tell her?" I demanded. "Tell me everything you said."

"I only spoke with her for a minute," Mom explained. "I just told her you'd been to the eye doctor, and that he said there's something wrong that's probably going to get worse. That you'll be having more trouble seeing as time goes on."

I leaped to my feet, aflame with anger. "Mother! You didn't! You had no right to tell anybody! How am I going to face the kids at school now? They'll all know!"

"They won't *all* know," Mom pleaded. "No one knows but Brenda."

"That's what you think! She'll broadcast it

to the whole world! You might as well put it on the six-o'clock news!"

"Look," Mom said wearily. "They'll have to know sooner or later. Once they understand, the other kids can help you in class if you need it, or show you where things are. They can give you a little extra consideration — "

"Yeah, sure! They'll give me consideration like they give it to Sheila McGraw!" Tears scalded my eyes, and I was shaking all over. "You're not even supposed to be too tall or too fat or too dumb or too smart! You've got to be normal in everything or else you're out of it, and you can never get back in no matter what!"

"Tracy, calm down — "

"How can I calm down? As long as nobody knew what was wrong with me I could still have friends, I could still make people think I was a regular person. And you had to go and ruin everything!"

Mom was silent. I rushed on, faster and wilder. "It was bad enough when I bumped into things and called people by the wrong names. Now you had to let everybody know I'm not just clumsy, I'm some kind of a freak!"

"Maybe Dr. Silverman is wrong," Mom said. "We don't really know anything yet." Before I could interrupt, she added, "Even if you do have this *retinitis pigmentosa* and it's incurable, you're not a freak. You can learn, and have friends, and do things — "

"Do things!" I repeated in disgust. "Like what things?"

"People that can't see well, they do all kinds of things you'd never think of. I've been re-membering a girl I knew in college, she used to swim laps every day."

"Yeah? And what else?"

"Oh. I don't know. Lots of things."

"Lots of things!" I muttered. "Like selling pencils on the corner, right? Sounds terrific."

For the first time Mom gave an exasperated sigh. "Tracy, don't be purposely difficult! I'm trying to talk about this in a reasonable way."

"There's no reasonable way to talk about it!" I exploded. "It's a disgusting, unfair thing and I don't know why it has to happen to me!"

Mom let go of the curtain cord, and for a moment it swung to and fro like a pendulum in the light of the window. "Lunch is almost ready, if you care to join us," she said, and marched to the door.

"I'm not hungry," I began. But she was gone, her footsteps lost down the carpeted stairs.

For a moment Sasha sat still, head up, star-ing at the closed door. Then she bounded to me, wagging her tail, and nudged my knee with an imploring paw. She gazed into my face as if she wanted to talk, and I could almost hear her questions. Why do we have to stay in here all the time? Why can't we go out and have fun?

Sasha leaped with joy when I got to my feet and went slowly to the mirror over my bureau. Red and bleary, my eyes stared out from my puffed face. My hair was a thicket of tangles. I snatched up my brush and tugged furiously at the knots, hardly wincing when they caught and pulled. How could my very own mother betray me? How could she hand over the secret I had guarded all these long months? The savage strokes of the brush echoed the word, *unfair! Unfair! Unfair!*

Through endless hours I had lain on my bed, trying to blot out the world. But now I boiled with anger. I banged the brush down and flung the door open so hard that it crashed against the wall. Sasha cavorted around my legs as I stamped down the hall to the bathroom and splashed cold water onto my face.

I'd have to go to school tomorrow. I'd have to face Brenda and Nancy and all the rest of them, with their stares and whispers. I'd have to endure Mrs. Blanchard's fussing, her insistence that I change my seat to sit nearer to the blackboard. And then I'd have to come home to this funereal house, where everyone acted as though I had just died.

Well, I wasn't dead yet. I was up and moving at last, hurtling toward whatever future stretched before me. There's nothing like getting good and mad, I discovered, to show you that you're still fiercely alive.

Chapter 11

For weeks Brenda and I hadn't walked to school together. But the next morning she was waiting for me when I passed her house.

"Hi!" she called. "I was afraid you were gone already!" Her big suede purse swung jauntily as she hurried to meet me.

"No, I'm still here." I rearranged my armload of books, trying to guess what was on her mind.

"I've got to get to school before the bell and tack up this poster for the Booster Club." She tapped a rolled-up paper tucked under one arm. "I was up till midnight working on the dumb thing, and it didn't come out right. It's ugly, and I mean ugly."

"I bet it's fantastic," I said. "Come on, let me see."

An odd, doubtful expression chased across

her face, and I realized I had said just the wrong thing. "Can you — uh — see well enough?" Brenda stammered. "I mean, your mother said you — "

"Oh, that." I tried to sound light and breezy. "It's no big deal. I can look at a poster, don't worry."

She hesitated before she set down her books and unfurled her masterpiece. I stepped closer to admire her fancy lettering. "There's nothing the matter with it," I protested. "It looks perfect to me."

"Sure," Brenda said, rolling the poster up again. "I guess you really can't see all that well, then."

She was only half kidding. I felt her eyes on me as we walked along, watching every move I made for signs of trouble. "How are things going with David?" I asked, to deflect her attention.

"We hung around his house for a while yesterday afternoon," she said. "His cousin was over and we wanted to fix you up with him. That's how come I called and talked to your mother." I winced, but she went on. "What really is happening with you? You've been acting so weird lately. Is it on account of this thing with your eyes?"

There was no taunt in her voice. She sounded

like she really wanted to understand. "I guess I have been doing some crazy things this year," I admitted. "I kept noticing that I couldn't see in dark places, stuff like that, and I didn't want everybody making a fuss about it, so I just tried to keep it to myself."

"Is it true, what your mother told me? Have you really got this awful disease of the eye?"

"That's what the doctor says." Did I only imagine that she edged a little away from me, as if RP might be contagious?

"But you still can see most things, can't you?" Brenda asked. "Like, you can see me when you talk to me, right?"

Now that she knew so much of the story, maybe it would be best to answer all of her questions, to bring everything into the open. I tried to explain it all, about seeing fine out here in the bright light, about the trouble I had at night and in dark rooms.

Brenda was silent a while, absorbing what I told her. "And it's going to get even worse?" she asked at last. "You won't even be able to see this much?"

I answered with a wordless nod. We turned onto Hancock Avenue, where the sidewalk began. Cars whooshed past, and the wind teased an empty paper bag ahead of us over the pavement. I was tired of talking about RP, but I couldn't think of anything fresh and interesting to say. Neither of us spoke until we reached the corner across the street from the school. Then, half-turning away from me, Brenda muttered, "I'd go crazy if I were going blind. I don't know how you stand it."

"I don't," I said. "I don't stand it at all."

There was a shout up ahead, and someone waved frantically from across the street. When we drew closer I saw that it was Nancy. "Brenda, did you do the poster?" she called. "Come on, we've got to put it up by the cafeteria."

"Have we got time?" Brenda asked. "Maybe we better wait till lunch."

"We can make it," Nancy insisted. "Dan's down there. We had a fight on the phone last night, and I don't want to face him by myself. You've got to come with me, Bren."

For the first time that morning Brenda gave her familiar laugh. "If you say so. Okay, let's go."

She glanced back and waved at me. " 'Bye, Tracy. See you," she called, and they disappeared into the crowd at the door.

We'd been drifting apart all year, I reminded myself, and it wasn't only because of my eyes. I wasn't always sure I wanted her for a friend.

Still, as I climbed the steps and pushed through the heavy front door, I felt very much alone.

The story of my eyes flew through the school all day, twisting farther from the truth with each retelling, like the message in the game of Telephone we used to play at birthday parties. When I walked into the gym, Sheila McGraw dashed up to me, shouting, "Tracy! You're still here! They said you were dying in the hospital!"

"No, I think I'll do that tomorrow," I said.

Sheila gazed at me, bewildered. "They were talking about it in study hall," she said. "They said the ambulance took you Friday night."

It was so bizarre that it was almost funny. "Well," I said, "let me know when you hear what my last words are. I hope I say something deep."

For a second Sheila didn't seem to get the joke. But she was grinning as she walked away.

For the first time in my life, I was a celebrity. People I didn't even know were discussing me across the aisles in study hall, in the cafeteria line, over hushed tables in the library. I, Tracy Newbury, was famous. But no, I realized, they were talking about someone they only imagined, the nobly fading heroine of an afternoon soap opera. Soon the melodrama would chip away to disclose the real Tracy, fumbling along in the dimming light. I wouldn't be interesting anymore. When they noticed me they would feel tense and uneasy, the way Brenda felt this morning. They would escape as quickly as they could to their own kind of people, normal people who only made normal mistakes.

Still, I felt a sense of relief by the time I reached home that afternoon. The long day was over. My dreaded secret was out to the world, and I had survived.

Craig's voice reached me above the din of barking as I started up our driveway. "Tracy!" he called. "Wait up!"

He sprinted across the road and caught up with me by the kennel door. "You want me to help you work Sasha this afternoon?"

"Sure!" I said eagerly. As we put Sasha through her obedience exercises, RP slipped into the background. She was in fine form this afternoon, gliding almost flawlessly through her routine as Craig played judge.

"She's improved a lot," he said when we finished. "I bet you could still enter that match in April. They're probably not filled up yet."

"No!" I said sharply. "I don't want to. I can't."

"Has it got something to do with all this stuff

they were saying around school today?" Craig asked slowly. "That's there's something wrong with your eyes?"

I nodded, sinking onto the couch. "I'd be tripping over my own feet in a show, especially if it's at night. I'd look like a complete jerk in front of all those people."

"You wouldn't," Craig said, but he didn't sound very convincing. "Is it really bad, like they were saying?"

"Depends which rumor you heard." I tried to laugh. "I'll live, anyway. But it's bad news for my eyesight. They don't know how long I've got."

"Maybe they'll find a cure," Craig said. "They can cure all kinds of things."

I wanted to believe him. Sometimes I even dared to hope that the specialist in Boston, whom I would see in a month, would know of some amazing new treatment. But deep down I knew Dr. Silverman was right. To medical science, RP was still a mystery.

"I don't know," I said. "I don't like to talk about it much."

Craig tried to shift the conversation to other topics. He told me about the trip his family planned to take during spring vacation, down to Washington, D.C. He said he'd like to spend the whole three days wandering through the

Smithsonian. But I couldn't think of much to say. After a while he said he had to go.

"Listen, Tracy," Craig said when I walked him to the door. "If there's anything I can do, any way I can help. . . ." He trailed off uncertainly.

"Thanks." Somehow I managed a smile. "You do help. Just by being here, hanging out the same as always."

"That's easy," Craig said, waving as he headed across the yard.

Upstairs Melissa began tuning her violin. At least, I thought, the house was getting back to normal.

But as I started up the stairs, Mom burst in the back door calling, "Tracy! You're home! Have you looked in your room yet?"

"I haven't been up there," I said. "Why?"

"Come and see." Mom led the way, stepping grandly aside when she reached my door. Mystified, I peered in past her shoulder. For a moment I couldn't fathom why she was so excited. Then I saw it — a brand-new stereo system arranged on my bookcase.

"Oh, Mom!" I cried, rushing over to get a closer look. "It's really neat! It's even nicer than Brenda's!"

"Your father and I decided last night that we wanted to buy it for you," Mom explained.

"Since you didn't have much of a Christmas this year — nothing exciting to open under the tree — "

"I already got Sasha," I protested. "She was my present."

"I know," she said. "But we wanted to give you this, too." She left the real reason unspoken in the air.

"Thanks so much," I said. "I love it."

I put on a Huey Lewis tape and tried to feel happy. But I knew the stereo was a sort of consolation prize. It would always remind me that I had RP.

I put on headsets so the music wouldn't bother Melissa, and assured Mom that the sound was perfect. "I'm running over to the store," she said, when she was certain everything was fine. "We're out of milk, and we need some dessert for supper."

I sat by myself, engulfed in the music. But I let the machine click off when the tape was over, and sat on my bed, too depressed to move. What was happening to me? I was coming apart, drifting away from my friends, losing interest in so many things that had been important to me.

Somehow I had to gather up the shattered bits of my life. I had to talk to someone who could understand.

Melissa was working on her Bartok piece, full of jaunty runs and sudden stops. It filtered down through the kitchen ceiling as I picked up the phone and punched the numbers: two-three-six, H-E-L-P.

"Crisis hotline, can we help you?" It was a man's voice this time, slow and questioning. I couldn't explain anything to this stranger. I was about to hang up, but somehow I collected my wits enough to ask, "Can I speak to Lynne?"

"Lynne? Sure. Hold on." I listened to a long pulsing silence. At last there was a click on the line, and a familiar voice said, "Hello?"

"Lynne!" I exclaimed. "Hi. This is Tracy, remember me?"

"Sure. How's everything going? School, your sister with the violin — "

"That stuff I told you about, it's going okay, I guess. I mean, that's not what I'm worried about."

"Well, what's really on your mind, then?" Lynne asked. She didn't even sound surprised.

I'd never get used to saying the words out loud. But I couldn't hide from them anymore. I drew a deep breath and plunged. "I just found out I'm going blind."

I pictured my words, crackling like flames

across the telephone wires. Lynne would stagger back, too appalled to reply. What could I expect her to say, after all? Nothing anyone said could stop my vision from fading.

"You just found out?" Lynne's voice sounded remarkably close, almost as though she had stepped into the kitchen beside me.

"Friday," I said. "It feels like it's been ages, though. This specialist says I've got something incurable that gets worse and worse."

"Is it *retinitis pigmentosa*?" Lynne asked.

"Yeah, that's what he called it. RP. How did you know?"

"It's not all that uncommon. Listen, I really think we should talk in person. I'd like to meet you."

"Why?" I demanded. "Can't we just talk on the phone? That's good enough."

"I think it would be better if you could come down to my office," Lynne said. "This is a tough thing for you to be going through, and the phone is kind of cold and detached — I'd really like to meet you."

The machinery of my mind ground slowly. I couldn't think of a good reason to say no. "Where's your office?" I asked.

"At Family and Children's Services in Millbrook. We're right downtown on East Third

Street, a block off Hancock Avenue. Could you come Thursday after school? Say around four?"

"Okay," I heard myself say. "I'll be there."

By phone or in person, Lynne couldn't really help me. But I had made a promise. On Thursday I would have to meet her face-to-face.

Chapter 12

Lynne's office was in an old brick house just down the hill from the Millbrook baseball field. I looked around furtively, terrified that someone might pass by and spot me. If anyone found out I was seeing a counselor, a new rumor would buzz through school — that Tracy Newbury was crazy.

But the street was empty except for a little girl pedaling a tricycle. Actually the house looked like most of the homes on the block, except for the grim sign above the door: FAMILY AND CHILDREN'S SERVICES.

A tall, thin woman ushered me inside. "Do you have an appointment?" she asked with a pasted-on smile.

"With Lynne," I said through the dryness in my throat. "She said to come at four."

"You're ten minutes early," the receptionist

said cheerfully. "Have a seat in the waiting room."

She pointed to a small square room off the entrance hall. I sat opposite a pale, middle-aged woman with frosted hair, who averted her face when I offered a smile. I wondered why she was here.

I didn't know why I was here myself. The waiting room brought back all the doctors' offices I had visited during the past weeks, and my heart thudded with dread. I wondered if the receptionist would go right on smiling if I leaped up and bolted for the door.

But if I broke this appointment, I might never dare to call the crisis hotline again. And I would need Lynne, whoever she was, in the months ahead. On the worst days her calm, steadying voice might be a lifeline.

What would she be like? I pictured her as tall and willowy, graceful, and light on her feet. She'd have blue eyes and a fair complexion, contrasting with her dark, flowing hair. . . .

I might be utterly wrong. She could be as old as Mom, with tired circles under her eyes from working so hard and frumpy clothes like Mrs. Blanchard wore. Suppose she turned out to be grotesque, with orange hair and ugly warts all over her face. . . .

Somewhere down the hall, a door clicked

open. I heard the murmur of voices and glimpsed a woman and a girl about my age as they headed to the front door. After a few moments the receptionist announced, "Miss Newbury, you may go in now."

I tried to think of myself as Miss Newbury, someone grown-up and sophisticated, fearlessly stepping forward to meet a mysterious stranger. I was on my feet, floating down the hall on a bubble of confidence, when someone emerged from the doorway and hurried toward me. She was a small, slight woman with flaming red hair, her face shining with a welcoming smile. In her right hand she carried a long white cane.

"Hi," she said. "Are you Tracy? I'm Lynne."

"You're Lynne?" I repeated. I couldn't help staring at the cane in her hand, but she didn't seem to notice.

"I really am," she said, laughing a little. "Come on in and have a seat."

Confident Miss Newbury was gone. I followed her into the office, timidly gazing around me at the pictures on the wall, the trailing philodendron that hung in the sunny window, the white cane that Lynne swung ahead of her with a steady tap, tap, tap.

She leaned the cane in a corner and circled around the desk, brushing it lightly with her fingertips. She smiled in my direction, but her eyes didn't quite find my face. I had the jarring sensation that she didn't see me at all.

"Sit down," she said, waving toward a chair. "Make yourself comfortable."

Obediently I dropped onto the chair. A long silence stretched between us, until I couldn't hold back any longer. "Lynne," I burst out, "are you blind?"

"Yes," she said, with the hint of a playful grin. "I am."

I stared, frozen with horror. She couldn't see me, couldn't see anything! It had really happened to her! She sat there calmly, living proof that the worst could befall me, too.

I felt like she had deceived me, taken me in. "Why didn't you ever tell me?" I demanded. "I've been talking to you all this time and you never said anything."

"We were talking about you, and what's going on in your life," Lynne said. "Most things about me weren't too relevant."

"I never even dreamed you were blind," I exclaimed. "You just sounded like — you know — like a regular person."

"Well, how is a blind person supposed to sound?" Lynne asked.

"I don't know," I floundered. "I guess that was a dumb thing to say."

"Not dumb, exactly," said Lynne. "Most people, if they've never known anyone who's blind, tend to think we must be pretty strange. Blindness seems like such a disaster to them, they figure it has to change your whole personality."

"It *is* a disaster!" I cried. "It's not like having a broken leg or a toothache, something that goes away."

Lynne turned suddenly serious. "Right now it seems like the worst thing that could happen to you. When I lost my sight, I thought I was going to lose my mind, too. But little by little I found out I could do most of the things I'd done before. I was the same person I'd always been."

"How did you go blind? How old were you? Can you really cross streets and everything just using that stick?" Maybe she hated to talk about it as much as I did. Maybe she'd get mad because I was so nosey. But I couldn't cut off the flood of questions.

Without hesitating, Lynne plunged into her own story. She had been twenty-one, she told me, in her senior year at college. Her blindness was a complication of diabetes. Over one devastating weekend she noticed misty spots hovering before her eyes, which grew larger and thicker until she could see nothing at all. She dropped out of school and spent a year at home, unspeakably miserable, convinced that her life was ruined.

I studied her all the time she talked. The blue flower print in her blouse was the same shade as the blue in her skirt. Her hair was combed, her lipstick was on straight. She could have been one of the younger teachers at school, or an office worker — any woman who held a responsible job. I wondered how she shopped for clothes and picked out combinations to wear.

How had she chosen the pictures for her office? There was a nice watercolor of an old farmhouse, an Audubon print of a ruffed grouse, and a photograph of two little girls on a seesaw. The room was pleasantly tidy, almost homey except for the big office desk. It wasn't the sort of place where you'd expect to find a blind person.

"Then finally our next-door neighbor told me about a friend of hers," Lynne was saying, "a blind woman who taught high-school biology. Our neighbor kept going on about how remarkable this woman was, so at first I didn't even want to meet her. I thought she'd just make me feel worse, doing all kinds of things I could never do. But eventually she came to see me, and we talked and talked. And I realized she wasn't a genius or anything. It was just that she had learned what she called 'the techniques of blindness,' — all sorts of ways for doing things that didn't require sight."

"What ways?" I asked. "What things did she do?"

Lynne cupped her chin in her hand, remembering. "Well, she sewed little Braille tags into her clothes so she'd know what color they were. She had Braille copies of the books her students were using, and she used models of amoebas and human cells and things like that instead of depending on drawings. And, what really impressed me at the time, she strung little bells on her son's shoelaces when he was a toddler, so she could hear where he was. It works, too — I found out with my kids."

"You have kids?" I couldn't take it all in.

"Two little girls. The ones in the photo over the desk."

"So after you met that teacher," I asked, "what did you do then?"

"I went to a rehabilitation center. You've got to live there for a couple of months. We learned how to cook and sew and iron and hammer nails and run an electric drill, you name it. And of course one of the main things was cane travel, learning to cross streets and take buses and find our way in unfamiliar places until we really got confident."

I thought of that night at Brenda's party, when I could barely find my way out of the basement. "I don't think I'd be able to do any of it," I said miserably. "I'd get lost in my own driveway. If I tried to iron I'd probably burn my hand off."

"Actually, I'm pretty lazy," Lynne said. "I'd rather buy things that are permanent-press."

We both laughed. There were still a hundred questions on my mind, and I rushed wildly ahead. "How do you cross the street?" I demanded. "You can't tell if the light is red or green."

"You use the cane to find the curb, and then you listen to the traffic. If it's flowing across in front of you, you know the light is against you. If the cars are going parallel to you, in the direction you want to go, then you're all set."

There was something else I needed to ask, but I didn't know how to shape it into words. "Even if you learn to do all these neat things," I began hesitantly, "what about people? You're still blind. They'll still treat you like — "

"Like a Martian," Lynne finished for me, and she didn't laugh this time. "It's true — that part never completely goes away. Most people who are blind will tell you dealing with people is the only really hard part."

"Now that everybody knows there's something wrong with my eyes, most of the kids at school act like — I don't know — like they don't know what to say to me. Sometimes they start shouting at me, 'Look out for the steps!', things like that. And this morning one of the boys stuck his hand in front of my face and said, 'How many fingers am I holding up?' "

"A lot of that will wear off," Lynne assured me. "After a while they'll get used to the idea that you get around all right, and things will go back to normal. But there might be a few people who just can't deal with it. That can be pretty painful."

"I'd rather hibernate in the house forever than go out with one of those canes," I said. "Everybody'd really be staring and whispering if I had to have one of them."

"I used to hate going out alone at first," Lynne said fervently. "I felt so clumsy and weird, I was sure I must look terrible. But finally I was going so crazy, sitting in the house day after day, I decided to brave it. After a while people got used to seeing me, and I got to where I could walk faster and feel a lot more graceful, so it was no big thing anymore."

"I don't need a cane, anyway," I said quickly. "I can see fine in the daytime, unless it's real overcast. And I don't really have to go out at night."

"You don't ever want to go out on a date?" Lynne asked, half-teasing.

"Well — maybe nobody'll ever ask me."

"They never will, if they get the message that you don't venture out after dark."

I felt trapped. A throbbing wave of panic rose in my chest. "But if I'm walking around with a cane, no one will want to go out with me then, either."

"It might be a little harder getting dates," Lynne said. "But your chances are a lot better if you're out there, doing things you like to do, showing people that you're an interesting, fun person."

I couldn't argue with her logic. But I couldn't bear the thought of taking one of those white canes to a dance or a movie. "Maybe my eyes won't get any worse than they are now," I said desperately. "The doctor said you can't predict what will happen with RP. And there might still be some new medicine we haven't heard about yet."

My words dropped like pebbles, disappearing into a deep, still pool with barely a ripple. Behind them lay a dense silence, so thick I didn't try to break through.

Lynne spoke at last, her voice low and a little sad. "In a way, RP is an especially cruel condition to have. It lets you get used to one level of vision, then it changes and you have to adjust all over again to a new loss. You have to live with uncertainty all the time, and that's incredibly hard."

I nodded, forgetting that Lynne couldn't see such a wordless gesture.

"But in a way there's a certain advantage," she went on thoughtfully. "You have years to deal with the fact that eventually you won't have much useful vision left. It doesn't hit you like a bolt out of the blue."

"But what if I can't adjust? Not even little by little?"

"You will," Lynne promised. "We humans have an incredible capacity to adapt to whatever comes our way. The thing is, don't overwhelm yourself worrying about the long-range possibilities. Just think one step at a time, day by day."

"Everything you say makes sense," I admitted. "I just can't quite believe it all. I guess I need time to think."

"You've got time," Lynne said. "Nothing drastic is going to happen tomorrow."

"I'm so glad I met you," I said as she walked me to the door. "I never knew a blind person could — you know — hold a job, have kids, have a regular life. It makes me feel like I shouldn't get so bummed out."

Lynne reached out and gave me a quick hug. "You'll do fine," she said. "Any time you want to talk again, just call me. I could even give you a couple of quick cane lessons sometime, just to give you the feel of it, if you're interested."

"I don't know about that," I said. "But thanks for everything. I didn't think talking to you could help. But it really does make a difference."

Chapter 13

As I walked home from Family and Children's Services, two voices waged war inside my head. Well, so what? the first one demanded bitterly. So what if Lynne managed to find a job and get married and have the kind of life you always wanted for yourself? You'll never begin to do the things she does. She's probably the only blind person in history who ever had it all!

But Lynne isn't the only one, challenged the other voice, softer, reassuring. There's that teacher she told you about, the one who tied bells to her son's shoes. Lynne said she wasn't brilliant, just practical. There must be other ordinary, practical blind people going about their business every day.

Oh, yeah? the bitter voice jeered. Where are

they, then? How come you never hear about them?

The softer voice was silent for a minute, defeated. Then it piped up excitedly. What about that girl Mom knew in college, the one who used to swim laps? Now that you're thinking about it, you'll hear of more and more people like that.

They're still just a few lucky ones, the angry, bitter voice insisted. If you end up going blind someday, forget it. You'll spend your life selling pencils, or sitting in a rocking chair. Maybe the Girl Scouts will come in and read to you.

Don't make things worse than they are, said the reassuring voice. Anyway, you might have your sight for years and years. Lynne is right — just take things one step at a time.

By the time I reached home, I felt as though I had spent the afternoon on a battlefront. I dropped to the floor to greet Sasha as she cavorted around me, but I was too exhausted to give her more than a few random pats. I sat motionless, leaning against the wall, while Lynne's words played and replayed through my mind.

For the first time since Dr. Silverman's diagnosis, someone had promised me that I could still be independent, could still live a rewarding life in spite of RP. But I would have to pay a cruel price. Little by little, I would have to find new ways of reading, identifying my clothes, moving about. I would have to stop pretending that I had normal vision, and learn all those useful, logical methods Lynne called "the techniques of blindness."

A key turned in the lock, and Melissa burst in. "Oh, Tracy!" she exclaimed, throwing her books onto the window seat. "I almost tripped over you! I didn't expect you to be sitting there like that."

"Sorry," I said, scrambling up. Melissa wasn't listening. In her hand she clutched the bundle of mail she had brought in from the porch. Swiftly she flipped through the pile, tossing aside bills and magazines until she stopped short, frozen, gazing at one long, brown envelope.

"It's here," she breathed, tearing at the flap.

"What is?" I asked, bewildered.

"My letter from Juilliard!" Melissa exclaimed. "This has to be my acceptance letter!"

The mangled envelope fluttered to the carpet, and Melissa unfolded the single sheet of paper. From where I stood, I could not see the expression on her face. I studied the taut muscles of her shoulders, the intent tilt of her head, and marveled that this moment must feel like the culmination of all her years of lessons and practice. I'd been hearing about Juilliard almost as long as I could remember — that shrine of a place where Melissa's teachers came from, where Melissa would go herself some day. . . .

Suddenly, as I watched, Melissa's whole body sagged. She caught at the armrest of the window seat and, in slow motion, collapsed in a heap beside her jumbled books. The letter slipped from her fingers to join the torn envelope on the floor, and I saw her face now. It was dead white.

"Melissa!" I cried, rushing forward. "What's the matter?"

She didn't answer, only pointed a trembling hand at the letter by her feet. I picked it up and began to read:

Dear Ms. Newbury:
After carefully reviewing your audition and your application material, we regret to inform you that we will be unable to admit you to our entering class . . .

I looked into Melissa's stunned, blank face. "You didn't get in?" I asked dazedly, still not absorbing the words I had just read.

"They regret to inform me," Melissa repeated. "They don't say what they didn't like, they don't say why I'm not good enough, they just regret to inform me. And that's it. That's all there is to it."

"Maybe there's a mistake. Maybe they got your application mixed up with somebody else's." I sounded as desperate as Dad when he started looking for specialists who might say Dr. Silverman was a quack.

She took back the letter and read it again, silently, shaking her head in disbelief. "It looks real, all right," she said, laying it down. "They're talking about me."

Melissa never cried. She swept through life, determined and efficient, and never had anything to cry about, as far as I could tell.

This couldn't be happening to my sister, to Melissa, who was so smart and talented, so pretty and charming, that people never told her no.

Slowly she got to her feet. She wavered for a moment, then headed for the stairs. "Melissa," I began, but she didn't turn around. Anyway, I couldn't remember what I'd wanted to say.

I went out to the kitchen and opened the refrigerator, but I had no appetite for a snack. How would Melissa break the news to Mom and Dad, I wondered. What would they say? Would Dad call up the school, demand that they reconsider. . . ?

The house was eerily quiet. Something was missing — Melissa hadn't begun to practice. Maybe she would never have the heart to play the violin again! The thought was unbearable. For almost as long as I could remember, I had played and done homework and daydreamed to Bach partitas and sonatas by Mozart. Silence in our house was all wrong.

I still didn't know what I wanted to say, but I found myself climbing the stairs. I paused on the landing, wrapped in that unnatural silence, and knocked timidly on Melissa's door.

With a twinge I recalled how I had told Melissa to go away when I had retreated to my room the weekend before. I braced myself for her to tell me to leave her alone, that I couldn't be of any help, but instead she called in a low, husky voice, "Come in."

She lay on her bed, huddled beneath a crocheted afghan. She pushed it aside and sat up as I came in, and I saw that her face was blotchy and streaked with tears.

"Can I — can I do anything?" I stumbled.

Melissa shook her head. "I just can't believe it," she said dully. "I guess I never let myself think I might not get in. And I thought my audition went really well. Nothing makes sense."

I sat at the foot of the bed. For a while neither of us spoke. With a jolt I realized that only an hour ago I had been in Lynne's office at Family and Children's Services. Now my own worries had slipped into the background. Melissa's grief seemed to fill up all the space between us.

"It's like the one thing I was aiming for just exploded, shattered into a thousand pieces," Melissa said, almost to herself. "I don't know which way I'm supposed to go now."

When I was miserable, Lynne always managed to turn me toward something hopeful again. "There are other music schools, aren't there?" I ventured. "There must be somewhere — "

"Sure there must," she said. "There must be lots of things — only I never thought about any of them much before." She mustered a feeble laugh. "Maybe I should think of this as a golden opportunity to try something new and different."

"Like what?" I asked.

"Beats me," Melissa said. "Got any ideas? You're the one who knows about choices."

I looked at her blankly. "What do you mean?"

"There was never any one thing you *had* to do. I've always been a little jealous of you, you know that?"

"Of me?" I exclaimed. "*You're* jealous of *me*?"

"What's so incredible about that? When you were little and people asked you what you wanted to be when you grew up, you changed your plans every other week. You were going to be a teacher or a cowgirl or a zookeeper or a ballerina. Anything might be possible. But *I* was always going to be a violinist — the best violinist around."

I couldn't figure Melissa out. But for the first time I suspected that we might not merely tolerate each other for the rest of our lives. Perhaps sometime we could become friends.

Melissa got to her feet. She took her violin from its case and ran her hands lovingly over the polished wood. "I think I'll practice," she said. "Any time I'm down, playing is the thing that helps the most."

I was halfway to the door when she called me back, sounding almost like herself again. "Hey, could you take this stack of mail back downstairs? I must have had it in my hand when I came up here, and I didn't even notice."

Strains of music, rich and warm, floated behind me as I descended the stairs. I glanced at the bunch of bills and advertisements in my hand. On top lay a thick, official-looking envelope from the Kittatinny Kennel Club. It was addressed to Ms. Tracy Newbury.

Puzzled, I tore the envelope open. Inside I found a glossy brochure about obedience regulations and a cover letter which began:

Dear Ms. Newbury:
We have received and approved your application to enter your dog, Hickory Road's Empress Sasha, in the Novice Class trial to be held on April 4. We must receive your application fee no later than February 23. . . .

There *had* to be a mistake this time. I had never sent in an application form. But somehow the Kennel Club had my name, and Sasha's, and they expected us to enter the Novice Class match. There must be an explanation — and suddenly I knew what it was.

Craig answered the phone on the second ring. "I told you I didn't want to enter her!" I exclaimed. "What did you do it for?"

"What are you talking about?" He tried to sound mystified, but he was laughing.

"You know what I'm talking about! You sent in the application for Sasha to enter that obedience competition, didn't you? After I told you I didn't want to go."

"Well — yeah," he confessed. "You're not mad, are you?"

"No. It's really nothing to be mad about, I guess."

To my own surprise, I actually felt a surge of appreciation as Craig went on, trying to explain. "I just thought — in case you changed your mind later on, you'd still have the chance."

"I can't do it," I said flatly. "It's at night. I'd probably step on some poor dog's tail, or fall head-first into the ring."

"Well, you don't have to go," Craig said. "You could just send them a note and say you're canceling out."

Somehow, his reaction was strangely disappointing. "I suppose so," I faltered. "Or just not send in my entry fee."

"That'd do it," Craig said. "No money, forget it."

"Sasha has been doing really well lately," I mused. "She'd probably be terrific. It's me who'd make a mess of things."

"Maybe the place'll be really well lit up," Craig ventured.

"Maybe it won't be. The ring should be okay, so everybody can see the action, but the rest of the place'll probably be dark as a dungeon."

"Even so," Craig said. "I bet you could manage. If you really want to, you can come up with a way to do it."

I thought of Lynne, and what she said about taking things one step at a time. Perhaps entering Sasha in the novice trial was the first step I had to take.

I drew a deep breath. "Okay," I said. "I'll enter. I don't know how, exactly, but I'll figure out some way to do it."

Chapter 14

"Keep an eye out for a parking space," Mom said from behind the wheel. She'd have to depend on Craig, I thought grimly. My view out the window looked like my idea of London fog. It was seven-thirty, and the sun was long gone. The streetlights cast shifting shadows, and downtown Flemington was a moonscape of canyons and tundra, a lost world without boundaries or reasons.

"Oh, here's one," Mom said brightly. "Looks like we're in luck tonight."

"I sure hope so," I said, glancing over at Craig. "The way Sasha's acting, we need all the luck we can get."

Ordinarily Sasha would sit contentedly in the backseat, intent on the scene that unrolled past the window. But tonight she wriggled onto the floor, tried to scramble into my lap, and finally attempted to jump in front beside Mom. At last Craig and I had managed to wedge her between us, but she whined and trembled with anticipation.

Mom got out first, and Sasha tried to vault after her over the back of the seat. I bent forward to grab her trailing leash, and nearly speared my face with the end of the white cane that stood between my feet. "I hate this darn thing!" I muttered. "It's going to kill me!"

"You really don't even need it," Mom said, peering in at us. "Why don't you just leave it in the car?"

Maybe she was right. Since the trouble with my eyes began, I'd been walking around without a cane, day and night. Lynne had taught me the basics of cane travel in a couple of lessons out on Third Street. But why should I begin to use a cane now, in public, with dozens of strangers watching me? The lighting might be fine in the civic center, where the show was to be held, and I'd feel like a jerk with my white stick in my hand.

Shoving the cane aside, I opened my door and stepped into the parking lot. Sasha bounded out behind me and lunged to the end of her leash. "Sasha, sit!" I ordered, giving her a no-nonsense tug. She sat reluctantly, but the leash almost quivered with her tension.

Here and there headlights wavered around me, like tiny buoys on a vast, dark sea. I stood still, not sure which way to go, waiting for some signal I could follow. Suppose the lighting inside wasn't much better! I'd be stumbling over everything, getting in everybody's way, making a hopeless fool of myself. I was right in the first place. I couldn't enter Sasha in an obedience match, especially one held at night!

One step at a time, Lynne had reminded me, as I practiced tapping my cane up and down the sidewalk. You have to begin somewhere, then take it day by day.

"Got everything?" Mom asked. In another second she would slam the car door, locking my cane safely out of reach. It would be too late to change my mind again.

"Wait!" I cried. I leaned back into the car and snatched up the cane from the floor. Today was the day I had chosen. This was the beginning.

"This way," Craig called. He was a moving shadow up ahead, weaving a zigzag path between the sleeping hulks that had to be parked cars. I stretched out my right arm and touched the pavement with the tip of the cane. Lynne had talked about a smooth rhythm, tapping the cane from side to side — and after a while as we worked together I had discovered what she meant. If I used it correctly, the cane would help me find a clear right of way, warning me of steps and curbs, posts and chairs, and table legs that I might not be able to see.

Now, with Mom and Craig and who knew how many other people looking on, I couldn't remember how to start. With panic swelling in my chest, I swept the cane in a wide, searching semicircle. It clattered against a car fender to my left, and I jumped back in dismay at the noise.

"Why don't you let me help you inside?" Mom asked. "You can hold my arm if you — "

"No," I said, more sharply than I intended. I couldn't walk in hanging onto my mother, as if I were a helpless little child. If I started letting people lead me around at night, I might never break away to move freely on my own.

Right foot forward, tap on the left side. Left foot forward, tap on the right. Right tap-left, left tap-right. That was it. The cane traced a low, narrow arc in front of me, just the width of my own body. Right tap-left, left tap-right, I followed the beacon of Craig's red jacket.

Sasha hauled ahead on the leash but I jerked her back and commanded her to heel. At least she wasn't trying to play with the cane, like she did last night when we practiced in the driveway. Right tap-left *thump!* The cane found something heavy and solid, a tire. I veered a bit to the right and went on toward the auditorium.

A wave of noise swelled out to engulf us when Craig pulled open the doors. Before my eyes could adjust to the artificial light, a dark form hurtled forward, there was a burst of snarling, and Sasha threw herself against my legs for protection.

"Patton, no! Quit!" a man's voice shouted.

Slowly they took shape in front of me — a burly, blond young man winding in a frantic Doberman pinscher at the end of a leash.

I bent to inspect Sasha — she was trembling with fright, but perfectly unscathed. My cane clattered to the floor as I gave her a comforting hug.

"I'm sorry," Patton's owner exclaimed. "I'll try to keep him out of your way — I mean, since you can't see him coming. He's not really vicious, but he's got this weird thing about shepherds."

How could I expect Sasha to perform in the ring after this? She'd be on guard with every dog she saw, ready to bolt and run at the first hint of danger.

I felt like bolting and running myself. The hall echoed with shouts and barking and the scrape of folding chairs. People talked in little clusters or hurried in a dozen random directions, and each human seemed to have a dog or two in tow. I would never find my way through the din and confusion!

But at the same time, I sensed that I had entered a world brimming with excitement. The room was like a giant stew, bubbling with dogs of every shape and variety. The light was bright enough for me to make out several of the nearest dogs clearly. Beside me stood two girls with identical toy dachshunds. An enormous St. Bernard loomed above them, panting like a locomotive. A white-haired lady scooped her yapping Pekingese into her arms, and a portly man in a business suit led in a roly-poly yellow Labrador. Everywhere dogs pranced and skidded, leashes crisscrossed, and owners feverishly sorted out the tangles. I wasn't the only person who looked confused, I realized with relief. In fact, chaos was part of the atmosphere.

"Hey, that's a real sweet little shepherd you've got there!" A gray-haired man stooped to give Sasha a pat. "I like that ear, gives her a rakish look, like a pirate."

An old friend of Mom's, who raised shepherds in Pennsylvania, came to join us. As we stood there, talking about dogs and training and past matches the others remembered, no one seemed much interested in my cane. I almost forgot about it myself. Our love of dogs bound us all together.

After a while Mom and her friend wandered away to watch the confirmation trials, which were already underway. Before I had time to wonder where I should go, a man rushed up to us and asked to see my registration card. "You're Novice A, over there," he said, pointing vaguely across the room. "I'm one of the stewards working that match. Here's your armband, so the judge'll know who you are."

I slipped on the narrow white armband. Our number, mine and Sasha's, stood out in bold black figures: 88. It was too late to back down now. They were expecting us.

There was enough light for me to see clearly the people and dogs nearby, but there was nowhere to stash my cane out of sight, and again I felt awkward and conspicuous. If only I could work magic and make the wretched thing disappear!

From this distance I couldn't see the ring, but I set off in the direction the steward had pointed. I struggled to conceal the cane behind my back with one hand and to make Sasha heel with the other. Craig stayed valiantly by my side, not even acting embarrassed to be seen in my company.

I had navigated half a dozen steps when something coiled around my left ankle and I tumbled forward. In the general hubbub, perhaps nobody heard my screech of surprise. But I made a definite impression on the woman whose lap I sprawled across, nearly knocking her off her chair. She gave an even louder shriek than I had, and let go of her dog's leash. The dog, a curly golden retriever, gave my face a reassuring lick before it dodged into the crowd.

"Belinda!" the woman screamed. Craig grabbed Belinda's trailing leash as she headed for the door. Belinda turned to leap up on her mistress, and Sasha decided the party had begun. She gave a delighted bark and wound her leash around me as she raced in a jubilant circle.

Something still dragged on my left ankle as I tried to work myself loose. "What in the world have I got?" I demanded.

"You hooked my backpack," explained Belinda's owner. "Your foot got caught in the strap."

We were all laughing as I untangled myself and handed her the canvas bag. The whole episode was like a bit of slapstick comedy. Still, when I unsnarled Sasha's leash and collected my cane, I felt more cautious about counting on my eyesight to get me to the ring.

As I stood there, wondering what to do, I was suddenly aware of Craig's questioning gaze upon me. "You want me to help you?" he asked, shyly holding out his hand.

Sure, I wanted to tell him. I need all the help I can get! Taking Craig's hand wouldn't be like letting my mother lead me around. People would hardly give us a second glance — they'd think we were boyfriend and girlfriend, drifting around in a blissful haze together. It might be nice to hold Craig's hand in mine. He had become such a good friend this year, I really did like him more and more. . . .

No. It wouldn't feel right. I couldn't pretend that something special had suddenly blossomed between Craig and me, when actually I was just hanging onto him so that I wouldn't trip over anyone else's backpack.

"That's okay," I told him. "I guess I better grit my teeth and try the cane again."

In this crowd I had to move slowly, even with the cane. I held it in close to me to avoid tripping anyone up, tapping only a foot or so ahead of me. Once I touched something soft that gave an exasperated canine groan, and once a woman hollered and jumped aside when I tapped her shoe. But I managed to remain upright, winding my way among the people and dogs and scattered folding chairs.

At last the ring widened out before me, a great empty and mercifully brightly lit oblong some forty feet wide, surrounded by low wooden fencing. "I think this is the place," Craig said. "Sasha, I hope you're in an obedient mood."

We were there just in time. "Will all entries in the Novice A Class match please come forward," called an official-sounding voice that made my stomach flutter. "All Novice A entries, come to Ring Two. The Novice A match is about to begin!"

Chapter 15

Looking over the eight of us, ranged along one side of the ring, I hardly noticed the people. The dogs were all that mattered. Beside Sasha sat a silky black cocker spaniel with such long ears I wondered how he could walk without stepping on them. There were two sheltys, a standard schnauzer, and a nervous-looking wirehaired terrier. The golden retriever called Belinda came to join us. And down at the end of the line sat Patton, the Doberman who had a thing about shepherds.

Sasha was so excited she ignored me the first time I told her to sit. Even when she was finally settled, she turned her head from side to side, trying to take in everything at once. Then she spotted Patton. She stared at him past all the other dogs, and he stared back. Even her floppy ear stood up almost straight as she strained to catch every whisper of trouble.

"This might be a disaster," I said to Craig in a low voice. "If that dog goes after Sasha again, what am I going to do?"

"His handler will stay on top of things," Craig said. "He's got him on a real tight leash."

"Yeah," I said, "but he'll be off leash in the ring. Then what?"

Craig gazed at the ceiling, as though the answer hung somewhere in the rafters. I patted Sasha reassuringly, and felt her muscles coiled tense and hard beneath her soft coat.

"All right," the steward called, raising his voice to be heard above the din in the room. "Let me quickly review what we'll do here tonight. As you know, the Novice Class competition consists of six exercises. I'll call each of you for the individual exercises: heel on leash, figure 8, stand for examination, heel free, and recall. Then you will all come into the ring together for the group exercise, what the rulebook calls the long sit."

"How's Sasha going to stay at sit with Patton glaring at her?" I asked Craig in despair. "Even if he doesn't go for her, she's so scared she'll probably make a break for it."

"Sasha," Craig said, bending to rub her ears. "You won't do that, will you? Who's scared of a skinny old Doberman, anyway?" Sasha licked his hand and went back to studying Patton.

"When I call your number, bring your dog into the ring on leash and get into position for the heel on leash exercise," the steward went on. "We'll start with Murray Hill's Dusky Midnight, Number 81."

The black cocker spaniel heaved himself to his feet. Led by a stout middle-aged woman with short graying hair, he entered the ring without tripping on his ears once. They walked to the end and turned to face the judge, Dusky Midnight sitting neatly at his mistress's left side.

They went through the exercises smoothly and efficiently. The cocker was almost too quiet and docile, I thought. He did everything he was supposed to do, but he seldom wagged his tail or showed any enthusiasm. He was well trained, but he wasn't much fun to watch.

Number 82 was one of the sheltys, Melbourne's Wandering Gypsy. She seemed to be doing fine at first, loping through the heel and figure 8 with her head high and tail waving. But when her handler stepped away from her for the recall exercise, Gypsy broke from her sit position and trotted after her. A groan of dismay ran along the ringside, and the judge rapped out, "Exercise finished!"

Gradually, as dog after dog entered the ring,

Sasha relaxed at my side. But even if Patton didn't give us trouble, how could I expect her to perform her routines in this raucous place, brimming with the scents of so many strange dogs? All along I'd been worried about myself, the showing I would make at a competition. I hadn't thought enough about what Sasha had to go through.

"Mayfair Farm's Jewel Belinda, Number 86," the steward called. Belinda was hardly a jewel in the ring. On the command to heel, she bounced into the air, caught the leash in her teeth, and gave it a playful shake. When the judge bent to examine her, she rolled onto her back, waiting for him to scratch her stomach.

"She's a little overly friendly," Belinda's mistress apologized.

"Exercise finished," was the judge's only reply.

Xanadu's General Patton came next. I had to admit he was a beautiful dog, loping into the ring with breathtaking grace. Head high, alert ears twitching, he glided through his performance, a picture of sleek, supple strength. He wasn't a clown like Belinda, or a bored robot like the black cocker. In the ring Patton carried himself with dignity and pride.

"Wow!" Craig breathed. "He's perfect!"

I touched the top of Sasha's head. Her gaze

was fastened on the dog in the ring. "He'll get a first," I said. "He's a real winner."

"Hickory Road's Empress Sasha, Number 88."

I was so absorbed in watching Patton that the steward's call caught me off guard. I jolted to my feet, and Sasha sprang to attention beside me, her body taut.

We stood only a few feet from the gate, and I could see no obstacles in my way. Wordlessly I handed my cane to Craig and led Sasha into the ring. Without hesitation she followed me to the end of the long rectangular enclosure and sat at my left side.

Relax, I told myself. It's going to be fine! I drew a deep, steadying breath and waited.

"Are you ready?" asked the judge.

Suppose I said no. Suppose I told him I needed a little more time to collect myself — say, five more minutes. . . .

"Yes, I'm ready," I said, my voice barely above a whisper.

"Forward," the judge ordered, and I relayed the command to Sasha. "Heel."

I had her total attention now. Watching every step I took, she trotted close by my left side, the leash hanging loosely between us. "Right turn," the judge ordered, and Sasha swung with me around to the right, never breaking her stride. The judge ordered us through the left turn and a complete about-face. He brought our pace from "slow" to "normal" and "fast," and still Sasha never lagged or tugged ahead, but flawlessly matched her steps to mine.

"Halt," the judge commanded. I stopped abruptly, and Sasha sat straight and tall at my left side, just as if she knew someone was keeping score.

Then it was time for the figure 8 portion of the exercise, when we had to weave a double circle in and out between two stewards. They took their places in the ring about eight feet apart and stood as motionless as pieces of furniture.

"Post," the first steward said cheerfully as Sasha and I approached. I must have looked as puzzled as I felt, but I heeled Sasha past her and up to the other steward.

"Post," the second steward announced when we were within two or three steps. Suddenly I understood. They had spotted my white cane, and they thought I couldn't see them, that they had to tell me exactly where they were. Would they think I was an impostor if they found out the truth, I wondered, completing the loop and heading back to the first "post" again. I stifled a giggle. I'd spent months pretending that I was fully sighted. And tonight, to avoid mix-ups, maybe I ought to pretend that I was fully blind.

"Exercise finished," the judge stated.

"Good girl," I told Sasha, giving her a warm pat. I hoped she understood how proud of her I felt. She hardly acknowledged my praise, just sat expectantly, waiting to learn what would happen next.

The judge wrote in his scorebook and looked up. "Stand your dog and leave when you are ready," he said simply.

I stooped and unclipped Sasha's leash, handing it to a steward, who stepped to my side. "Stay," I commanded, and walked away from her, resisting the temptation to glance at her over my shoulder. I stopped a few feet away and turned back to face her. Sasha's ears were back and her tail was down. She looked worried, as though her confidence were ebbing away. Still she stood firm when the judge approached and ran his hand lightly over her head, body, and hindquarters. The examination lasted only a moment, before he rose and ordered, "Back to your dog."

Like every exercise, this one had to be done in the proper form. The handler was required to walk around behind the dog and end at the dog's right, with the dog standing in the heel position. But as I approached her, Sasha could bear the wait no longer. She broke from her rigid "stay" and burst forward to greet me, wagging her tail in relief.

A titter of amusement ran through the crowd at ringside, and I felt my face flush. I wanted to apologize the way Belinda's mistress had, but there was no room for extra words. "Exercise finished," the judge declared, making another note.

There was no time to wonder how many points he had deducted from our score. I had to think of the next exercise — the heel free.

We started flawlessly. Again Sasha followed me through the right and left turns, gliding along by my side as if she thought I could still control her with the leash. Then, just as the judge stepped our pace up from "slow" to "normal," a racket of snarling and barking broke out somewhere off to the left of the ring. I tried to ignore the commotion, hoping Sasha would do the same, but it was too much to ask. She turned her head sharply, then lagged behind me as she stared off toward the noise. In icy panic I imagined her lunging for the gate and hurtling into the fray — but no, I had underestimated her. As the barking died down she quickened her pace and caught up with me, trotting through the rest of the routine as though nothing had happened.

The last of the individual exercises was the recall. Again I told Sasha to stay, turned, and walked away from her. This time I walked nearly the whole length of the ring before I turned back to face her. "Call your dog," the judge ordered, and I called, "Sasha, come."

I held my breath as she trotted toward me, willing her to remember the rules. This was no time for a joyful greeting. Even a pat on the head was forbidden until the exercise was completed. She must not even touch me with her nose.

Sasha didn't have the fluid grace of a dog like Patton. But she looked almost elegant as she drew nearer, her head held high, her body forming one smooth, flowing line to the waving tip of her tail. To my amazement she came to a halt directly in front of me and waited, just as we had practiced at home.

"Finish," the judge said briskly. At my command Sasha circled behind me and sat straight at my left side. I thought I heard a spark of admiration in the judge's voice this time when he said, "Exercise finished."

"She really did very well for her first match," Mom said when I led Sasha out of the ring.

"And you're handling her beautifully, Tracy! You looked so relaxed, as if you've been doing this all your life."

Mom's praise spread a warm glow all through me. Then Craig added to my exhilaration. "You did great!" he cried. "Even when that fight started — she hardly got distracted at all!" He crouched beside Sasha and gave her a big hug.

"You think so? Really? She messed up in the stand for examination, and she'll lose points for looking over at that fight — "

"So what?" Craig broke in. "If she didn't pay attention to that racket, she'd have to be sleep-walking. And you were so calm yourself, you never even flinched."

"All participants please enter the ring for the group exercises," called one of the stewards. "Line up along the far side, and leave plenty of space between your dogs."

"Got to go," I said, gripping Sasha's leash a little tighter. "Here comes the real challenge!"

Chapter 16

In the minute or two of confusion, with handlers jockeying their dogs into place, I maneuvered Sasha to a spot at the end of the line, as far as possible from Patton. At last a steward collected the leashes and the judge asked, "Are you ready? Sit your dogs."

Eight voices mingled, echoing the command over and over: "Midnight, sit . . . Belinda . . . Patton. . . ."

"Sasha, sit," I said in a low voice that I hoped rang with authority. She sat, and we waited again.

"Leave your dogs," the judge commanded.

Again voices rippled along the line: "Stay . . . stay . . . stay . . ." and slowly I was walking away, crossing the ring to watch and wait. For one long minute none of us could move.

At first Sasha kept her gaze fastened upon

me, and I began to think that we would be all right. If the dogs all concentrated on their own handlers, they would have no energy to waste on one another.

Then I saw Sasha's ears twitch. She shifted her position — not getting up, but definitely turning her whole body — and I thought fleetingly how the judge would disapprove, knock even more points off her score. In the next instant I looked where she was looking. Patton was no longer at sit. He crouched low to the floor, the hair bristling along his back, and even over the yapping of a dog across the room, I thought I heard a menacing growl.

I'd call Sasha, get her over to me where I could protect her. No, I should jump up and run to her, get between her and Patton. But Mom always warned me never to put myself in the middle of a dog fight, I wouldn't be able to help and I'd only get hurt . . . Dizzying thoughts sped through my mind so fast I couldn't grasp any one of them.

Suddenly Patton uttered a fierce bark, exploded from his place in the line, and flew at Sasha in a whirling blur.

"Patton! No! Quit!" The burly blond handler dashed across the ring as the obedient line of dogs turned into a bounding, barking melee. Most of the barks sounded playful, most of the tails seemed to be wagging with delirious excitement — but all control was abandoned, shattered into a glorious romp.

At last I found my voice. "Sasha!" I shouted. "Sasha, come!" I couldn't see her in the whirl of tails and ears and plunging bodies. She'd probably jump over the fence and try to get as far away from Patton as she could. This was no romp for him — he meant business. "Sasha! *Sasha!*"

"She's here!" Craig yelled from somewhere beyond the gate. "The steward's got her by the collar!"

I stepped over the fence and ran around the outside of the ring, avoiding most of the fray. Sasha threw herself toward me and I knelt beside her, hugging her in relief. She was trembling with fright and excitement, but she didn't have a scratch on her. She was safe.

Patton's handler had captured him and held him on a tight leash. "He's never done anything like this before," his handler told the steward. "He was fine in obedience class — "

"He'll have to be excused from the match," the steward said, shaking his head. "And we've got to send a report about this to the American Kennel Club. It may affect his eligibility for other trials."

For a second I thought the handler was going

to bristle up the way Patton did. But instead of arguing he turned away and half-dragged Patton from the ring. "I'm sorry," he told me, swerving past Sasha on his way to the door. "I don't know what got into him. He just has this weird thing about not liking shepherds."

By now the dogs in the ring had all been apprehended. Tongues lolling, they panted over the excitement while their frazzled owners stood by. "We'll do the group exercise again," the steward announced blandly, as though this were all a matter of course. "You'll have five minutes to get your dogs calmed down."

"I think I'd better take Sasha home," I said. Her trembling had subsided a little, but I was starting to feel pretty shaky myself.

"These things happen," Mom tried to assure me. "I've seen real fights break out, where dogs actually get hurt. Sasha'll be fine."

"If you pull her out now, you'll never know how she'd really do," Craig added. "She hasn't had a fair chance yet."

Sasha rested her head on my lap and closed her eyes as I scratched her behind the ears. Already she seemed to have forgotten her panic, now that Patton was gone.

"If she isn't afraid to go into the ring again," I decided, "we'll try it. If she acts scared, if she's cowering and holding back, I'm not going to force her."

"You wait," Craig said. "She's going to surprise you. I've just got this feeling."

For the first time I realized he was still holding my cane. I wondered if he felt embarrassed when people gave him questioning glances. But he didn't seem to mind. Craig wasn't the kind of guy who got embarrassed easily.

"All right," the steward called at last. "Bring your dogs back into the ring."

I got unsteadily to my feet and hesitated, trying to gauge Sasha's reaction. She rose, too, and stood by my side, head cocked. "You ready, girl?" I asked. "I'm not sure I am — but let's go."

Smoothly and quietly, never lagging, she followed me at heel and took her position once more in the line of dogs at the side of the ring. "Sit your dogs," the judge ordered once more, and at my command Sasha sat.

One minute. Sixty seconds. I ticked them by in my head as I watched Sasha from across the ring. *Ten . . . eleven . . . twelve . . .* She turned her head, alert to every movement in the row of dogs, but her body stayed firmly in position. She looked splendid, floppy ear and all.

Twenty-three . . . twenty-four . . . I caught a glimmer of movement at the far end of the line, and saw one of the sheltys inching its way closer to Midnight. Midnight didn't even turn his head.

Thirty-five . . . thirty-six . . . thirty-seven . . . Sasha's ears flicked forward. She was listening, focusing in on some sound I couldn't catch. I willed her to hold still, to put every thought out of her head.

From out of nowhere came a resounding crash. My nerves were so taut that I jumped, my heart racing. Sasha's head came up sharply, and I was sure she would break for the gate again. If I could just explain to her that it was the door slamming, nothing to be scared of — but I could only hope, and count the seconds. *Forty-seven . . . forty-eight . . . forty-nine . . . fifty . . .*

The judge stood impassive, studying the row of dogs. He must make mental notes of every shift and wriggle, subtract points each time a dog edged toward its neighbor with a glint of mischief in its eye. I didn't care if Sasha won a ribbon — it was enough that she sat so staunchly immovable after the trauma she had been through. I'd never dreamed she could do so well.

Fifty-eight . . . fifty-nine . . . sixty!

"Back to your dogs," the judge commanded, breaking the spell. I realized I had been standing as statue-still as Sasha was, but now I could move at last. Trying not to hurry, not to seem excited, I crossed the ring, walked around behind Sasha, and stood with her in the heel position beside me. I didn't care how many points the judge took off when she tilted her muzzle up to lick my hand.

"Exercise finished!" the judge announced. I felt like cheering. It was over! We had made it, both of us, Sasha and I.

"Good girl!" I told her fervently as I clipped her leash to her collar. As though she knew the show was over, Sasha jumped up on me, wagging her tail.

"I knew she'd be fine," Craig exclaimed as we left the ring. "Did you see how that one shelty kept wiggling around — but Sasha looked like she was above it all, she wanted no part of that stuff."

"She was fine, really excellent," Mom agreed. "I won't be surprised if she places, at least."

I'd never heard Mom speak of Sasha in that tone before. I knew my dog wasn't a disappointment any longer, a collection of undesirable traits cropping up after generations of near-perfect ancestors. Sasha was smart, and she had spirit. Even Mom admired her for that.

"I wonder what the judge is thinking," Craig

said. "He's sure going over his notes carefully."

"You think he'll give Sasha any extra points for combat stress?" I asked, giggling.

"That's not in the rule-book," Mom said. "They go by the rules, no matter what."

At last the judge and the stewards turned to face the little crowd clustered beside the ring. Voices hushed as the judge cleared his throat and began, "In the Novice Class, dogs can be awarded a maximum of two hundred points. Each exercise is judged separately and the points are totaled up to give the final score. Today the first prize, the blue ribbon, will be awarded to Murray Hill's Dusky Midnight, with a total score of 196 points."

"That dog did everything right," Craig whispered. "I don't know how he even lost four points, unless it was for looking like a wind-up toy."

"The second prize, the red ribbon, goes to Kendall's Bavarian Cream, with a total of 193 points," the judge continued. The woman with the standard schnauzer stepped forward to claim her prize.

"And in third place," the judge went on, "for a yellow ribbon, with a score of 190, we have Hickory Road's Empress Sasha!"

"You won!" Craig cried. "Third prize. That's fantastic!" Before I could absorb what was happening, he grabbed my hands and whirled me around in a joyful dance.

We were all laughing and talking at once when the steward presented me with Sasha's yellow ribbon. I turned it over and my mother read the words aloud: "OBEDIENCE TRIAL, 3rd prize, Kittatinny Kennel Club, Flemington, New Jersey." Here it was — tangible proof that all our work had paid off. But oddly, I wasn't as excited as I might have been about Sasha's ribbon. Something in me knew that this was only a beginning.

"You may as well give the cane back to me," I told Craig as we started for the door. "I might need it again."

Leaving the match was a slow process. Belinda's mistress stopped to congratulate me, and two shepherd fanciers gushed that Sasha was a credit to her breed. Mom paused to say good-bye to her friend from Pennsylvania, and when Craig and I got restless we told her we'd meet her by the car.

It was good to put the turmoil of the show behind us. But darkness engulfed me as soon as we stepped outside, and a few raindrops pattered on my hair. Almost automatically this time, I extended my cane and tapped it ahead of me as we crossed the parking lot. There was no sign of Mom, and after a minute or two we wandered away from the car, out onto an empty downtown street.

"You know," I told Craig, "I haven't felt this happy in months. Not since the beginning of school."

"You mean, on account of your eyes?" Craig asked.

"That was bumming me out for a long time," I admitted. "And — I don't know — everything seemed like it was messed up for a while. Nothing could go right, you know?"

Craig stopped in a little oasis of light in front of an all-night diner. "And now it's better?" he asked.

"I hope so — I mean, I'm pretty sure." We were standing close together, huddled in that pool of light, and I felt him looking at me hard. There was something I suddenly longed to tell him, but the words kept getting away from me. And if I didn't find them now, as we stood here so happy and close, I might never have a chance to say them at all.

"If it weren't for you, I wouldn't be here right now," I fumbled. "You sent in my application, you talked me into entering — no, it's more than that. You never act any different, whether I'm wearing glasses or walking around with a cane. Just as if I hadn't changed at all."

"You haven't changed," Craig said. "You're

the same person you've always been — and I like you fine the way you are."

My heart was racing again, even faster than when I went back into the ring with Sasha. Then plop! A big raindrop splashed onto my forehead. Another landed on the tip of my nose and trickled down my cheek. Sasha shook herself vigorously, splattering my slacks with flying drops. Off in the distance thunder rolled — the first thunder of the season — and suddenly rain pounded down on us as though someone had ripped open the clouds.

"It's pouring!" Craig cried. "We'd better run for it!"

I gripped my cane and started after him, water pouring onto my face and down my neck. "Don't worry about your cane, come on!" Craig exclaimed. In one smooth gesture he took the cane from me and seized my hand. I didn't argue this time. I knew he wasn't just trying to help me because I couldn't see very well.

"We're going to get soaked!" I cried.

"Can you swim?" Craig asked. "We might have to, the way it looks!"

Laughing, we ran through the pelting rain back to the car, hand in hand all the way.

About the Author

Deborah Kent grew up in Little Falls, New Jersey, where she was the first blind student to attend the local public school. She received a B.A. in English from Oberlin College and an M.S.W. from Smith College School for Social Work. After spending four years as a social worker at the University Settlement in New York City, she decided to pursue her lifelong dream of becoming a writer. In the town of San Miguel de Allende, Mexico, she found a colony of American writers who offered invaluable criticism and encouraged her to complete her first book.

Ms. Kent has written several novels for young adults, as well as nonfiction children's books and many articles in the field of disability. She lives in Chicago with her daughter Janna and her husband, R. Conrad Stein, who is also the author of many books for children.

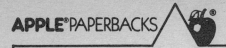